FIC   Bush, Maureen
BUS   Feather brain

Date Due

ORCA
YOUNG
READERS

Feather Brain

Maureen Bush

ECOLE MILL BAY

ORCA BOOK PUBLISHERS

Library and Archives Canada Cataloguing in Publication

Bush, Maureen A. (Maureen Averil), 1960-
Feather Brain / written by Maureen Bush.

(Orca young readers)
ISBN 978-1-55143-877-1

1. Dinosaurs--Juvenile fiction. I. Title. II. Series.

PS8603.U825F42 2008   jC813'.6   C2007-906963-0

First published in the United States, 2008
Library of Congress Control Number: 2007940945

Summary: Lucas gets more than he bargained for when
he orders a dinosaur-making kit off the Internet.

Orca Book Publishers gratefully acknowledges the support for its publishing programs
provided by the following agencies: the Government of Canada through the Book
Publishing Industry Development Program and the Canada Council for the Arts,
and the Province of British Columbia through the
BC Arts Council and the Book Publishing Tax Credit.

Typesetting by Bruce Collins
Cover artwork by Eric Orchard
Author photo by Barb Yates, Helen Scott Studios

ORCA BOOK PUBLISHERS
PO Box 5626, STN. B
VICTORIA, BC CANADA
V8R 6S4

ORCA BOOK PUBLISHERS
PO Box 468
CUSTER, WA USA
98240-0468

www.orcabook.com
Printed and bound in Canada.

12 11 10 09 • 6 5 4 3

For Mark, Adriene and Lia.
Thanks for keeping me laughing.

Acknowledgments

I'd like to thank Brian Cooley and Mary Ann Wilson for their wonderful book *Make-a-Saurus: My Life with Raptors and Other Dinosaurs*, the inspiration for *Feather Brain*.

Thanks to Sarah Harvey for pulling my story out of the slush pile, for the fastest-ever acceptance and for such a careful and gentle edit.

And many thanks to everyone at Orca for the wonderful work they do.

Contents

CHAPTER 1   Make-a-Saurus 1

CHAPTER 2   Stegy 11

CHAPTER 3   Feather Brain 25

CHAPTER 4   The Beast Attacks 34

CHAPTER 5   Get Rid of It! 46

CHAPTER 6   Dinosaurs at the Zoo 54

CHAPTER 7   The Cat Came Back. 64

CHAPTER 8   To Catch a Thief 72

CHAPTER 9   Parley 80

CHAPTER 10   The Monster from the Lagoon 90

CHAPTER 11   howweirdcanyouget.com 104

CHAPTER 12   Onion Breath. 112

CHAPTER 1

Make-a-Saurus

"Lucas, mail for you," Mom called up the stairs.

"One of my packages?"

"Both!"

"All right," I yelled. I bolted down the stairs and skidded to a halt at the front door.

Our postie stood on the doorstep, snow melting on her shoulders, holding out two damp packages. Both were addressed to me, Lucas Clarke, in Calgary, Alberta. One was in a big flat envelope; the other, perched on top, was about the size of a large milk carton.

"Something special?" she asked.

"Birthday presents," I said, taking them from her. "I mean, I ordered them with birthday money. They're for making dinosaurs."

1

She grinned. "Show me when you're done?"

"Sure," I said.

She walked down the sidewalk, leaving tracks in the wet snow. It was the second Wednesday in March, two weeks after my tenth birthday, and I'd been dying for these packages to come.

I sat on the stairs and tugged open the envelope. It held a thin book: *Make-a-Saurus: My Life with Raptors and Other Dinosaurs*, by Brian Cooley and Mary Ann Wilson. Dinosaur models leapt off the cover—a wire model, a clay one and a finished dinosaur, complete with feathers and teeth and claws. It looked totally real.

I started turning pages, getting more and more excited. The book showed how Brian Cooley makes dinosaur models. Then it explained how kids could make them too.

"Good book?" Mom asked, sitting beside me on the bottom step.

"Look at this, Mom. It's awesome." I flipped through the book, describing everything.

She laughed. "You've had it for five minutes and you're already an expert?" She ruffled my hair. We both have red hair—mine short and bright, hers long and dark. "What's in the box?"

I was so excited about the book I'd forgotten about the other package—the dinosaur-making kit. Together, they'd be incredible!

I tore open the box and pulled out a handful of scrunched-up paper. Then another and another. Was there anything inside?

Finally I found it—one small glass test tube filled with clear liquid, topped with a cork stopper. It was sealed in a ziplock bag, along with a small piece of paper. I held up the bag. "This is it? This is supposed to be a dinosaur-making kit?!"

Mom bit her lip. "I hate to say I told you so, but…"

I groaned. "I know. You said, 'You never know what you'll get when you order off the Internet.' But the ad looked so good!" I groaned again, dropped the test tube into the box and stuffed all the paper back on top. What a waste of twenty bucks. At least the book was great.

I headed up to my room and flopped onto my bed to read. I didn't stop until I'd finished the book. It was amazing; I couldn't wait to get started. I grabbed a pad of paper and a pencil and started listing all the things I'd need.

The dinosaur on the cover was a sinornithosaurus (pronounced sigh-nor-nih-tho-*sore*-us, according to Brian Cooley). It's one of the feathered dinosaurs from

China. That was what I really wanted to make, but I decided to do something easier for a trial run. I glanced out the window. Fat lazy snowflakes drifted down. Maybe I'd make a fat lazy herbivore.

I turned back to my list. I'd need wire for the frame. We had wire cutters and masking tape, and I had lots of scraps of colored foam sheets I could use for padding. We had newspaper for papier-mâché, and I had lots of paint.

I decided to make a stegosaurus and cover it with poppy seeds for the skin texture. I'd need something to use for teeth—what would work for that? What about the spikes for the tail? And the plates that stick out of his back—what could I make those with? Maybe if I wandered through the craft store I'd get some ideas.

I wrote out everything I needed. Then I put down my pad with a grin. I'd talk Mom or Dad into taking me to the mall tomorrow.

I spotted the other package where I'd dropped it on my table. Slowly, I unpacked the test tube again. There wasn't much in it; the test tube was no bigger around than my pinky. The liquid was as clear as water, although it moved more slowly when I shook it. What was I supposed to do with it? I unfolded the piece of paper tucked in the bag:

Make A Dinosaur Come To Life

Mix the solution with your papier-mâché goop (glue or flour paste) and make a papier-mâché dinosaur. There is enough for three small projects or one large. You will be astounded at how lifelike your dinosaur will become for you. But be warned: what you create is yours for life unless it is stolen from you.
www.howweirdcanyouget.com

And that was it. Weird was right. What a waste of money. I stuffed the paper and the test tube back in the box and tossed the box under my table. Then I dashed downstairs with my list.

Mom took me to the mall after school on Thursday. It was snowing again. Mom shook snow off herself and brushed snow off my hair as we walked into the mall. I'd already found something for dinosaur teeth when I was walking to school that morning. Gravel had been spread over the roads when they were icy. I kicked the snow away and picked out a dozen small rocks the same shape as my back teeth, but much smaller.

I found a white comb at the dollar store for spikes on the tail, but nothing for the plates along the back of the stegosaurus.

Mom had to buy some birthday cards, so she left me at the craft store with orders to meet her at the card shop when I was done. I wandered all through the store: yarn, embroidery floss, beads in tubes not much bigger than my dinosaur-kit test tube, pipe cleaners. I found wire, but nothing for back plates. I kept wandering. I could cut colored foam sheets into the shape I needed, but they'd be soft. Some scientists think the plates on stegosauruses were soft, for heating and cooling instead of for defense, but that didn't sound very exciting.

What would be hard enough? Cardboard, wood. What about the wooden cutout pieces? I rummaged through the bags: teddy bears, flowers, leaves, hearts. Come on! Why not just plain triangles? Then I took another look at the hearts. If I set them in upside down, there'd be just a point showing. That would work!

Fishing in my jacket pocket for the money Mom had given me, I carried the wire and the bag of wooden hearts to the front desk. I counted out five dollars and looked around while the clerk rang it up. A kid with shaggy blond hair was leaning against a pillar outside the store. I held my breath. Let it not be Kyle, I prayed, let it be anyone but Kyle! He turned; I groaned. It was Kyle.

He was the meanest boy in my class, maybe even in all of grade four, and he especially hated me. He'd hated me ever since I first came to the school last September. "Red curls?" he'd said, looking me over. "Hey, Lucas has girly curls." Which is why I keep my hair short, too short to curl. But Kyle always finds something to bug me about.

I turned my back and hunched over the counter. There was no way I wanted him to know I was buying hearts! When the clerk handed me my bag, I took a deep breath and tried to look tough as I sauntered out of the store.

Kyle stepped right in front of me. He was taller and heavier than me, and he knew it. "Shopping in the craft store, Clarke? What a girl!"

I flushed and tried to stuff the bag into my pocket. I could feel the little wooden hearts sending out flashing messages: *Clarke bought wooden hearts. Clarke bought wooden hearts.*

I swear Kyle heard them. He reached for the bag. "What have you got in there?"

I pulled it back, close to my chest. He grabbed at it, tearing the bag.

I pushed him away. "Back off, Kyle. What I buy is none of your business." I sounded tough, but I could feel my face becoming as red as my hair. Of course Kyle noticed.

He imitated me, in a high-pitched voice, "'What I buy is none of your business.'"

I just turned and walked away, clutching my bag and thanking the Great Stegosaurus in the Sky that Kyle hadn't seen those wooden hearts.

I checked over my shoulder to make sure he wasn't following me and smacked straight into Mom. She caught me, and then checked to see what I'd been looking at.

"Is that a boy from school you were talking to? Why don't you invite him over? You should have friends over sometimes."

"It's okay, Mom," I said. "I see him at school all the time. I'd rather just work on my models at home." In fact, Kyle was the reason I never invited anyone over. He was the reason I had no friends at all. No one dared to be friends with me, not with Kyle around.

But I really did like working on my models. As soon as I got home, I cleared off my table. I have a work table under my window, instead of a desk, for making models. Under the table are three plastic boxes full of dinosaur-making supplies. Finished models live all around my room, on the shelves and hanging from the ceiling. I also have dinosaur footprints on the floor and dinosaur posters on the walls.

The book said to start with a sketch. I searched through all my dinosaur books until I found a good side view of a stegosaurus skeleton, and I made a rough sketch from that. Then I pulled out the wire to start the frame.

I checked the book again. It said, "To make two hind legs and two arms, just make the same limb twice, except in mirror image. You don't want a dinosaur with two right hind legs, otherwise it will walk around in circles!" I laughed. If I could have a dinosaur that walked, I wouldn't mind if it walked in circles.

But I didn't laugh much after that. Working with wire is nasty. I had five scratches and two holes in my fingers by bedtime. And my dinosaur still kept falling on its nose.

I got up early Friday morning, threw on some clothes and worked until Mom made me come down for breakfast. At least she didn't complain when I gulped down my cereal and ran back to my room. By the time I had to leave for school, I finally had a frame I liked. I walked to school happy, even though I had to trudge through six inches of wet snow.

After school I pulled out a bag of colored foam bits and started padding the dinosaur. The legs were easy; I just imagined elephant legs. But the body was awful. I struggled to make it big enough without it looking like a fat lump.

I had to pad it a bit but not shape it totally, because I'd be adding papier-mâché. I didn't put any foam on the head. Stegosauruses had really small heads and tiny brains. I figured wire and papier-mâché would be enough for that.

When I was done, it looked like some lumpy multi-colored weirdness, not like a dinosaur at all. How could this possibly work?

CHAPTER 2

Stegy

Dad rented a video for Friday night so I wouldn't disappear into my bedroom right after dinner. Saturday after breakfast, Mom made me clean my room and do my homework. Then Dad insisted I help him shovel the walks, which took forever because the snow was so deep. We both groaned about spring in Calgary. At least the sun came out, and it was warm.

By afternoon, they were ready to leave me alone, and I got to work. I tore up strips of paper, filled a red plastic tub with water and set it on an old towel on the table. I pulled out a green plastic bowl and half filled it with water. Then I searched for my white glue.

While I was groping around in my plastic boxes, I spotted the dinosaur-making kit behind them. Should I use it? Why bother, I thought as I straightened up with the glue in my hand. I opened the top and turned the glue bottle upside down over the bowl. The dinosaur kit was just junk. My hand tightened in anger, and a huge blob of glue oozed out and blorped into the water. I groaned. That was way too much. I stirred it in with a paint brush; it was definitely too thick.

I glared down at the kit. "It's all your fault," I muttered. "Maybe I will use you, just to thin out my gloop." I grabbed the box, yanked out all the packing paper and pulled the test tube out of the bag. I was going to dump it all in. Then I remembered the note said it could make one large or three small projects, so I slowed myself down and poured carefully. I was hoping it would do something interesting, like smoke or bubble, but all it did was drip. I poured one-third of the liquid into the bowl, stuffed the cork back into the test tube and stirred the potion into the watery glue. It was still too thick. I slowly added water until it was just the right consistency.

All afternoon I dipped newspaper strips in the watery glue and carefully wrapped them around my model. Soon I had sticky water dripping off my elbows, paper bits stuck to the back of my hands, and an itchy nose I didn't dare scratch. I rubbed it on my sleeve and kept working.

Once I'd finished the first layer, I cut slits in the wet papier-mâché. I wasn't sure if I should do it right away or when the paper was dry, but if I waited and was wrong, I couldn't go back. I cut the slits with scissors and set in the wooden hearts, upside down so only the pointy part stuck out. My dinosaur books couldn't agree on whether the plates pointed straight up or if they alternated, pointing up to the left and then up to the right, all down the spine, so I picked alternating because I thought it would look good. Then I set the dinosaur on the windowsill to dry.

It wasn't ready for another layer of papier-mâché until Sunday morning. I did a second, thinner coat and left it in the sun to dry while Mom, Dad and I went tobogganing.

We walked down to Confederation Park, all layered up in ski jackets and pants and boots, not because it was cold, but because the snow was melting and we knew we'd get soaked. Dad picked a north-facing slope because the snow was already gone in patches on the sunny side of the park.

We had an awesome time, whipping down the hill. The snow was really fast because it was so wet. When we hit the bottom, water sprayed all around us. Then we got cold—the wind had a bite to it, and it cut through our wet clothes right to the skin. We didn't care. This was probably our last chance before spring really took hold, and we didn't want to waste it.

Until Kyle arrived. He roared down the hill, not caring who was below him, blasting past us with a whoop. I tugged my toque down over my hair, hoping he wouldn't recognize me. But Mom's long red braid was bouncing against her back. He seemed to hate red hair. What if he recognized hers?

"Let's go," I said as we slowed at the bottom. I wanted to be walking away before Kyle headed back up the hill. "I'm wet, and I can't wait for some hot chocolate."

Mom and Dad glanced at each other, surprised at such a sudden change. Then they shrugged and smiled at me.

"Sure, hon, whatever you want," Mom said.

Dad chased me while Mom pulled the toboggan behind us. I dashed up the hill out of the park, glancing over my shoulder. Kyle was trudging up the slope, looking down. He hadn't seen me!

We came home soaked, red-cheeked and happy. After changing into dry clothes and warming up with mugs of Dad's special hot chocolate, I went upstairs to add one more layer of papier-mâché. I shaped the head, creating eyebrows and a nose, and then I thickened the legs at the knees.

When I was done, I set it out to dry while I worked on my homework. As soon as I got *Make-a-Saurus*, I knew I had to use it for my book report. The kids in my class liked dinosaurs; I figured they'd love this report. And Kyle couldn't stop it, not with our teacher there.

On Monday I wore my dark green dinosaur T-shirt, the one with a picture of a dinosaur skeleton in the middle and *Paleontologist in Training* written underneath. And I brought *Make-a-Saurus* and my almost-finished stegosaurus. On the way to school I named him Stegy.

I'd wanted to bring a finished model, but it turned out bringing a partially done one was a better way to explain the book. The whole class seemed interested, even Kyle, except he tried to hide it. I could tell everyone liked it by the silence, and by their eyes—intent on me, my T-shirt, the book and Stegy. But when it was time for questions, Kyle crossed his arms and glowered, and suddenly everyone was looking down.

My teacher, Miss Dubois, said, "What? No questions? I thought you guys would be bursting with them after such an interesting book report."

Kyle shot rays of hate out of his eyes at me. Everyone else kept their eyes glued to their desks. So Miss Dubois asked a couple of questions; then I sat down.

I was so mad. I could tell by the glances from the kids around me that they were really interested in Stegy. I sat and stroked his back. I carefully packed him in my backpack at recess so no one could take a look while I wasn't there. If they didn't have the guts to disobey Kyle, I wasn't going to let them touch Stegy.

After school, Kyle stood on the steps, glowering at anyone who glanced my way. Stegy and I walked home alone.

I went right back to work on Stegy when I got home. He'd be great, and no one at school would ever see him again!

I cut four large teeth from the comb for spikes on the tail, putting my anger into every cut. I hate Kyle—*snip*. I hate Kyle—*snip*. When I picked up Stegy I calmed down; I wasn't angry with him. I used a big needle to poke holes for the spikes and glued the spikes into place. Using the tip of my scissors, I dug out larger holes in his mouth and glued in bits of gravel for teeth. Then I glued on some googly eyes, the kind that rattle when you shake them.

I got the jar of poppy seeds Mom said was in the back of the fridge and used a paintbrush to coat Stegy in glue. Carefully, I sprinkled poppy seeds onto the wet glue, but I should have worked on one section at a time. The glue dried too fast, and I had to put on more glue near places poppy seeds were already sticking. Soon I had poppy seeds in my glue and glue in the poppy seeds. I guess the extras weren't going back in the fridge! Eventually, Stegy was all gray from little seeds, and I could soak my brush and hands to clean up while the glue dried.

After supper I dug out my paint, four paintbrushes of different sizes, a cup for water and a roll of paper towels. I flipped through my books until I found a colored stegosaurus painting I really liked and set to work.

I started by painting most of the body green. While the paint dried, I worked on my spelling list. Then I used beige paint, mostly along the spine, with some trickling down between the back plates. I let it dry another hour while I finished a page of math and had a shower. Just before bed I pulled out the red paint. I painted red edges on the back plates and red stripes on the white spikes. I added a little red around the mouth and below the eyes and set him to dry overnight.

In the morning I painted the toes black and added a touch of black around the mouth. He looked awesome! He was a bit lumpy, like Mr. Garner across the street, but I didn't care.

I took Stegy down to breakfast so Mom and Dad could admire him and not be mad about the gluey jar of poppy seeds. Mom just laughed and added poppy seeds to the shopping list. She said I could leave Stegy in the middle of the table as a centerpiece, but I took him back to my room. I set him in the middle of my table—he was my best model ever.

I raced to school, thrilled by how well Stegy had turned out. It finally felt like spring: warm and gentle. Most of the grass was still dull brown from the winter, but I could see little bits of green around the bases of trees.

In class, I put up my hand to tell Miss Dubois I'd finished Stegy, and I described how I'd done it. She grinned and asked the class if they'd like me to bring him in. But Kyle cleared his throat and hunched his shoulders, and everyone kept their eyes down and their mouths shut.

Every moment of free time, all day, Kyle stalked around, his eyes narrowed, looking for the right moment to torment me. No one dared ask about Stegy.

I dragged myself through the rest of the day and slipped out quickly after school. The sun was gone, the sky was gray and the wind was cold and biting. I pulled my jacket close around me and hurried home, shivering.

I raced upstairs to check on Stegy and slid to a halt in the middle of my room. He wasn't where I'd left him on the table. Had Mom cleaned my room and moved him? Slowly I turned, looking on every surface in the room. Where was he?

Then I spotted him, behind the dinosaur-kit box I'd left on the corner of the table. "How did you get there?" I muttered as I picked him up. Then I dropped him right back down on the table. He was warm. I glanced out the window; the sky was dark with clouds. "How could you be warm?" I asked.

I picked him up again and gasped. He was moving! Not from me picking him up, but…from breathing? I held him in my hands and stared. His sides really were moving, very slightly, in and out, in and out. He looked better than when I'd made him, leaner and stronger somehow. And more real. This was weird.

As I started to set him down, he turned his head and looked at me. I yelped and dropped him. How could he be alive? I reached out to touch him and he spun away from me and swung his tail. I snatched back my hand; those spikes were a lot sharper than teeth from a comb!

I knelt and looked at him. He stared back. I held out my hand, slowly, and laid it on the table in front of him. He looked at me, and then he stepped up to my hand. He sniffed it, stepped back and gazed at me. I smiled. "Hi," I said.

He turned away. I watched him walk all around the table top, stopping to sniff at everything. When he got to the plastic bowl, he leaned in and licked the water pooled in the bottom.

"Are you thirsty?" I asked. "Of course you are. Probably hungry too."

I glanced around my room. What would a stegosaurus eat? Plants. There wasn't much green in the garden yet. Maybe I could raid the fridge.

I raced downstairs, slipped into the kitchen and grabbed a bowl of water and a handful of lettuce leaves. Then I ran upstairs, so excited I could hardly breathe. As I stepped into my room, I closed my door. I didn't want anyone to know about this!

"Hey, Stegy," I said in a soft voice. He backed away from me, tail waving. I walked up to him, holding out a lettuce leaf in one hand and the water in the other.

I set the bowl on the table with the leaf beside it and stood back. Stegy watched me for a moment and then stepped toward the water. He sniffed and bent down for a long drink. He drank again; then he looked up at me, still wary.

"Go on, try the lettuce," I said. I knew he didn't understand me, but he nibbled an edge and then settled down to eat. He ate slowly, chewing carefully just like Mom says I should. He kept going, only stopping when every bit of lettuce was gone. Then he went back to exploring the table.

When he got too near the edge, I picked him up. He growled and swung his tail. I grabbed it and lowered him to the floor. Then I let go and jumped back. "I just thought you'd like to explore some more," I said. "And I don't want you falling off the table."

I put the water down near him and sat on my bed to watch. Slowly, he checked out my whole room. He sniffed at my shoes; then he disappeared under my bed and came out dusty and sneezing. I gave him a ball to play with, but he wasn't sure what to do with it.

Mom knocked and, before I could say anything, opened the door. I spun around to block her view of Stegy sniffing the ball. "Dinner's ready. Have you done your homework yet?"

"I—uh—don't have much—just my spelling list. I'll do it after supper."

"Okay. Come on down."

"Yeah, I'll be there in a minute." I waited until she closed the door. Then I turned back to Stegy. "I have to go now, but I'll be back soon. And I'll bring you something more to eat." Stegy snorted gently against the side of the ball. I patted him and left, closing my door behind me.

For the first time in my life, I asked for more vegetables at dinner. I'd grabbed a Baggie and sat with it tucked between my legs. Whenever my parents looked away, I dropped something into the bag. Spoonfuls of corn. Cooked carrots. Chunks of potatoes.

Mom was astounded. "When did you start to eat vegetables?"

I just grinned and squirmed. "I don't know. Are potatoes vegetables?"

Dad laughed and served me more. "Yes, they are."

Stegy didn't think much of cooked food. I had to sneak down for raw carrots and more lettuce before he'd eat again.

Wednesday after school I took Stegy out to play. White clouds raced across the sky, and sunshine warmed our backs. I carried Stegy into the backyard, where lots of snow had melted, and let him graze on the little bits of bright green grass around the apple tree at the back of the garden. He chowed down on the grass, eating all the green spears. Then he kept going, grazing on dried grass. I lay back, propped on one elbow, and watched him. It was a bit like having a tiny pet cow.

"Hi, Lucas," called my dad. I sat up with a jerk. He came striding across the lawn, too fast for me to hide Stegy. I just sat there, stunned. This was my secret. I didn't want anyone else to know!

Dad sat beside me and as he sat, he grabbed Stegy. "Wow, he looks so good!"

I reached out for Stegy, knowing Dad would drop him as soon as he realized he was alive.

But Dad hung on. He turned Stegy over, examining him carefully. "This is cool. You did an incredible job. I'm really proud of you."

I just sat there, open mouthed, waiting.

"You should take it to school, to class. I bet lots of kids would be interested in how you did it."

Yeah, right, I thought. Not with Kyle around.

Dad put Stegy back on the ground, jumped up and turned away. "Dinner in half an hour," he called over his shoulder.

I sat staring. How could he not have noticed? I looked down at Stegy. He glanced up at me and then turned back to grazing. I thought about what Stegy had done when Dad was here—nothing. Absolutely nothing. He hadn't moved at all. Was I the only one who could see him alive?

Just before dinner, I took Stegy back upstairs. I made sure he had water. Then I pulled out the dinosaur kit and shook the test tube gently. *Enough for three small projects.* I grinned and read the directions again, muttering. "'You will be astounded at how lifelike your dinosaur will become for you. But be warned: what you create is yours for life unless it is stolen from you.'"

I sure was astounded! I kind of liked the part about him being mine for life; why would that need to be a warning? This was the best birthday present ever! And I wasn't going to share him with anyone. Not ever! As I went down for dinner, I shut my door and hung a sign on my doorknob:

Special Project Underway
Do Not Enter

CHAPTER 3

Feather Brain

On Thursday I put on another dinosaur T-shirt: white with three feathered dinosaurs on the front. Maybe that would get the other kids talking to me. If they knew about Stegy, they'd all want to be my friends, but I wasn't about to share him. Not now. Besides, I wasn't sure who else could see that he was alive. If any adult knew what I had, I was pretty sure they wouldn't let me keep him.

It was cool in the schoolyard before the bell rang, but I took my jacket off anyway, to show off my T-shirt. A couple of guys gathered around to look at it. I started to describe the recent discoveries about feathered dinosaurs. They were really interested, until Kyle arrived.

He swaggered up in his too-big black jacket, blue eyes snapping as he realized kids were talking to me.

"Hey, Clarke!" he called out, standing just beyond the circle of kids. They turned at his voice and slowly drew back from me, leaving me alone to face Kyle.

He stood with the sun behind him; I squinted up at him, trying to see his face.

"What's that on your T-shirt? Feathered dinosaurs?" He laughed. "Yeah, right. Dinosaurs fly? Only a feather brain would come up with something that stupid."

He grinned and looked around. The other kids shuffled their feet, but no one told him he was the feather brain.

"Let's see. Lucas Clarke. Luke Clarke. Lark! Hey, Lark! Hey, Feather Brain!"

I knew he wanted me to take a swing at him, but I just stood there, totally still. I told myself that he was the idiot, that I was bigger than this. But my face gave me away. I could feel the flush start at my neck and surge up into my face.

Kyle grinned; he knew he'd won. "Hey, what's that on your face, Lark?" He leaned closer to me. "Those spots—are they—are they splashes of bird crud?" He flicked my cheek with one finger.

Freckles—he was talking about my freckles! I turned bright red, my face matching my hair. Kyle laughed and sauntered off, and all the kids slipped away while I stood flaming in embarrassment.

I spent the day feeling angry and humiliated. Kyle's the idiot, I thought over and over all day. No one would look me in the eye, and they all stayed away from me at recess and lunch. After school I stomped home in fury.

I knew I'd have friends if it weren't for Kyle. Every step home I muttered, "I hate Kyle. I hate Kyle. I hate Kyle!"

As soon as I got home, I started to work on a new dinosaur. This time I wasn't going to make a nice little grass eater, a placid cow. I wanted something fierce, something nasty, something strong enough to take on Kyle.

I sketched in great dark slashes and cut wire with a chant for every snip. I hate Kyle—*snip*. I hate Kyle—*snip*.

This time I was making a sinornithosaurus. I had to double-check how to pronounce it: Sigh-nor-nih-tho-**sore**-us. It meant Chinese reptile bird. But what it really meant was *Eat your words, Kyle*. I'd show him he didn't know anything about feathered dinosaurs. I was going to make a nasty, carnivorous, feathered dinosaur, take it to school and teach the whole class how wrong Kyle was.

I used the model in *Make-a-Saurus* to base my sketch on, so I could move on to the wire structure really quickly. It was easier this time. I had a better idea of how to work with the wire, and I was so mad I didn't mind getting poked. I just rubbed away the blood and kept working all Thursday evening and every moment I could on Friday.

I struggled to get the limbs just right to support the body; it kept falling over. Stegy wandered over, curious. I pushed him away. I needed to concentrate. I kept at it until it would stand, but then it looked too tame. I wanted something wild, like on the cover of the book. I looked carefully at the picture and adjusted my model, trying to imagine it covered in papier-mâché and painted. Finally, I had it. It looked ferocious— absolutely perfect.

I worked all weekend. Saturday morning I wrapped it in layers of foam, much thinner than for Stegy. Then I made up more papier-mâché goop, carefully dripping in exactly half of the liquid left in my test tube. Hands shaking, I slowly stirred it into the glue-and-water mix. I felt great, like I was creating life.

I tore the paper into thinner strips and went more slowly than I had with Stegy. It had to be just right. This time I took Brian Cooley's suggestion about using dryer lint for details like shaping the shoulders, eyelids and throat. Mom didn't even blink when I told her what I wanted. She's used to my projects.

Saturday afternoon I set the sinornithosaurus in the sun on the windowsill to dry. I opened the window to a warm breeze. The world was still brown, with only a few bits of green grass showing, but it felt like spring.

"Stegy, do you want to go outside?" I asked. He gazed up at me, dark eyes gleaming. I smiled and picked him up. A lot of my anger at Kyle had been used up in making the sinornithosaurus.

I took Stegy out to the front garden. First he grazed on the new grass along the edge of the front flower bed. Then he wandered into the bed and began eating the tips of crocus bulbs. It looked like he loved them; he settled in for a long, slow dinner.

Then he put his head down and grunted. I wasn't sure why, until I clued in. He was pooping. My first thought was, Oh, gross! but that was immediately followed by, Coprolites! I have my own coprolites. That's dinosaur poop. Of course, I quickly learned the difference between fossilized dinosaur poop and the fresh stuff. But still, dinosaur poop!

I sat, warm in the sun, enjoying Stegy and his poop, until Kyle came by.

"Playing with your cow, Feather Brain?" he called from the sidewalk. "Moo, moo!" He doubled over, laughing.

I glanced at Stegy; he was motionless, just a model.

Mom walked around the corner of the house, holding a pruning saw in gloved hands, bits of leaves clinging to her long red hair.

Kyle stopped suddenly and stared at Mom. When she smiled at him, he looked startled; he slowly smiled back. Then he turned to me, his face still. "See you later, Clarke," he said as he turned and walked away.

Mom watched Kyle leave; then she looked at me sitting on the grass with Stegy. She squatted near me, folded up her pruning saw and tugged off her leather gloves.

"I worry about you, Lucas," she said, touching my head. "Always alone. Why didn't you invite your friend in? You never have friends over, not since we moved here. You do know they're welcome, don't you? Even if I'm working when you get home, I won't mind."

"I know, Mom," I said. "He's not someone I want to get to know better."

"Is there anyone else? You really need a friend."

I squirmed. Sure, I thought, but with Kyle around I'll never have one. I sighed. It wasn't like I could tell her, *Mom, Kyle hates me, and everyone else is afraid of him, so they can't be my friends.* My stomach knotted around the words. Mom would be horrified. She'd march straight to the school—and all that would happen is that Kyle would hate me even more.

"I'll see, Mom," I said. "I do hang out with kids at school—in class and at recess."

"Okay," she said, smiling. She patted Stegy and stood. Then she saw the crocuses, tips chewed right down to the dirt. "Look at these! They were just coming up—the first flowers of the year. They look like they've been eaten!" She scowled, looking around the yard for the culprit.

I pushed Stegy behind me. "I saw a rabbit crossing the street early this morning," I said, hoping to divert her.

She scowled again and stomped off, muttering about rabbit stew.

Sunday morning I painted my sinornithosaurus brown. I planned to add details around the face and nails later; first, I needed a basecoat.

I spent all afternoon fussing with the details. I cut the small teeth off my white comb for dinosaur teeth and carefully set in each one. But what could I use for toenails? I sat fiddling with the comb, wondering if a black one might work. Then I remembered the feathers I'd bought on Saturday. I dumped out the bag on my bed and picked out the largest feathers. Carefully I cut off all the long, dark ends and set them into my sinornithosaurus's feet. They looked wicked—sharp and curving.

Feathering the dinosaur was absolutely the worst part. First I had to sort the feathers. I laid them out on my bed by size and color. Then I had to arrange them all over again when a gust of wind from the open window scattered them across my room.

I had to glue them on in rows, starting at the bottom of the legs and along the belly, then slowly working up the body. Feathers stuck to the glue on my fingers and flew up my nose. I kept rubbing my itchy nose on my sleeve and ended up with glue on my nose and feathers on my sleeve.

Finally, I was done. Monday morning before school I did the final paint touchup, mostly black around the toes and eyes. Then I set it on the windowsill to dry completely and raced to school. I'd never felt happier. I knew nothing Kyle could do would touch me; I was invincible.

It was a beautiful day. Somehow Kyle must have known he wouldn't be able to get to me, because he left me alone, even at recess. I talked to a couple of guys about dinosaurs and told them more about my new book. They admired my black T-shirt with the growling glow-in-the-dark dinosaur head. It's my *Don't Mess With Me* T-shirt, and it worked.

I was happy all day. After school I shot out the door. I couldn't wait to get home.

CHAPTER 4

The Beast Attacks

As soon as I stepped into the house, Mom stormed out of her office, a sheaf of tax papers forgotten in one hand. "Lucas! Lucas Clarke! I want to talk to you!"

Oh, no! Had she found Stegy? I put down my backpack with a thump and slipped off my runners, watching her out of the corner of my eye.

"Your room is a complete mess! I brought up your clean laundry, and your room is a disaster! I didn't even try to clean it up. If you want your room to be private, there are going to be some rules! Number one: KEEP IT CLEAN. Number two: Bring your dirty laundry to the laundry room every morning. Number three: No food in your room. Number four: Put away your clean laundry. Is that perfectly clear?"

I stood there, petrified. Of her, of course—my mom's scary when she's mad. Maybe I should sic her on Kyle! But even more than that, I was petrified that she had seen something—what if she found out Stegy was alive?

I squeaked, "Sorry, Mom. Yeah, I'll clean it all up and I'll follow the rules. I promise."

She stomped back into her office, looking disappointed she couldn't yell at me anymore, and I raced upstairs. My room wasn't that bad, was it?

It was. It was totally trashed: bedding dragged off the bed, pillow spewing feathers, models knocked off the shelves. What had happened? The sinornithosaurus was sitting on the windowsill, just where I'd left him, facing the window. Where was Stegy? Could he have done all this?

I searched my room and finally found him under my table, cowering inside the dinosaur-kit box. The edge was damaged; it looked like it had been chewed. I reached inside to pull Stegy out. He roared and growled.

"Hey, it's okay," I said in a soft voice. I laid my hand inside the box so he could sniff it. "It's just me. What have you been doing? My room is a total mess. How could you do this all by yourself?" While I spoke, I slid my hand under his belly and pulled him forward.

Then something hit my back. I dropped Stegy and leapt up, but whatever it was clung to me, scratching and clawing. I screamed and shook it loose. I could hear it drop to the floor behind me. I spun around, and my new sinornithosaurus reared up on the rug, screeching. He launched himself at me again, raking his claws down my arm. I grabbed a book and beat him back. When he was on the floor on the far side of the bed, I dashed out the door, slamming it behind me. I leaned against it, panting, while he screamed and clawed at the door. What had I done?

I remembered how hungry Stegy had been the first day and how thirsty he was. Maybe the sinornithosaurus was hungry. I dashed downstairs and checked out the fridge. Cheese, milk, bread. He was a carnivore. Was there any meat? I found some sliced roast beef for sandwiches. I grabbed five slices, some lettuce for Stegy, a bowl and a glass of water. Then I crept back up the stairs, hoping Mom wouldn't see me taking food up.

"Lucas, what's with all the noise?" Mom called from her office.

"I'm practicing something for school," I said, praying she wouldn't get up from her desk.

"Just keep it to a dull roar, would you?"

Usually I hate tax season, when Mom is too busy for anything but work, but for once I was thankful her desk was piled high with tax forms.

The scratches on my back stung as I slipped upstairs. I paused at the door, listening to figure out if it was safe to go in. I heard thumping, then shrieks. Stegy!!! I'd forgotten about him!

I yanked open the door and rushed into the room, sloshing water onto my socks. The sinornithosaurus was rearing and hissing, his teeth viciously sharp, his claws like daggers. Stegy was cornered—head down, plates deflecting the blows. I was so glad I'd made them strong! Stegy turned and swung his tail at the beast. He landed a hit I could hear, a huge thump. The spikes dragged down the beast's front leg. The beast shrieked and backed off, blood beading along the cut. They stood panting, staring at each other.

I dropped the meat into the bowl, put it on the floor and used a book to push it close to the beast. Stegy stayed on the alert, tail swishing. The beast jerked his head to the side for a moment and then again as he sniffed. He backed away from Stegy, strode over to the bowl and lunged at the meat.

He didn't really eat it; he ripped and tore and dismembered it, meat hanging from his mouth, bits flying when he shook pieces to tear them. It reminded me of nature shows where lions tear antelopes apart. Except this was smaller and on my bedroom rug. My stomach heaved. There was no way I was eating meat for dinner.

Once the beast had devoured the meat, I poured some water into the bowl. He lapped it up. Then he lay down beside the bowl with a sigh and fell asleep.

He looked kind of sweet sleeping.

I carried Stegy outside to eat, away from the beast. By the time he'd grazed for half an hour on new grass, he'd stopped shaking. I hadn't.

The beast slept all evening. I pushed him over to the wall so I wouldn't bump into him by accident; then I made a safe nest for Stegy inside the dinosaur-kit box. Then I went to bed, wondering how I was going to cope with two dinosaur pets.

I didn't sleep long. In the middle of the night, something landed on my head with a screech. I threw up my hands and yanked it off; it was the beast. He didn't like being grabbed. He attacked, teeth and claws scratching my face and tearing my pajamas. I leapt out of bed, trying to beat him off with my pillow. Feathers flew across the room. Finally, I pinned him between my pillow and the bed. I scooped him up with the pillow, flung the beast and the pillow into my closet and slammed the doors shut.

He launched himself at the doors, roaring and screeching. I could hear his claws raking down the wood. I pushed my dresser in front of the closet doors, pinning them shut. I didn't want that thing escaping.

I didn't sleep again. I lay in bed, listening to every bump and howl, all the scratches on my body stinging. What was I going to do?

What I finally did was slide meat on a plastic lid under the closet doors twice every day. I used a straw to fill another plastic lid with water. I wore the same jeans for two weeks because I didn't dare go into my closet for clean ones. I wore long-sleeved shirts every day. I figured Mom and Dad and Miss Dubois would be okay with scratches on my hands, but if they saw my arms, they'd start to ask questions. And I put a new sign on my door:

Special Project Under Way
Private
Stay Out
Mom and Dad, this means you!
I know the rules

Every day when I fed the beast, he scrabbled to get at my fingers under the closet doors. And every day I had to get a new straw after he attacked and shredded the one I was using. I could've just let him starve and die of thirst, but that seemed too cruel, even for a monster.

Sometimes he'd pull the plastic lids too far away for me to reach; then I'd have to send in a new one. After a while my room began to smell of rotting meat and dinosaur poop, but I didn't dare go into the closet to clean it up.

I learned to turn on my radio whenever I fed him or whenever he was noisy, which was a lot of the time. Otherwise Mom or Dad would bang on the door and ask exactly what my special project involved.

"Just practicing dinosaur cries," I said.

Stegy became quieter and quieter. The only time he seemed happy was when I took him outside. He loved grazing on fresh grass and the shoots of plants coming up in the garden.

I learned to like being at school more than being at home. That was weird. Even Kyle didn't seem so awful.

And then, one Friday morning, I couldn't find my jeans. I'd been dropping them on the floor every night and pulling them on again in the morning. But they were gone. The closet was still blocked by my dresser, so the beast couldn't have done it. Stegy was snoring in his box. Mom? Oh, no—laundry!

I raced downstairs. Sure enough, my jeans were whirling around in the washer in a flurry of soap bubbles. I looked down. I was wearing pajamas; little dinosaurs danced down my legs. Definitely not for Kyle's eyes. Could I convince Mom I was sick?

"You'll have to wear something else today," her voice announced from behind me. I spun around.

She smiled. "Your jeans will be clean and dry tomorrow. Today you need to choose something else." She pushed me toward the stairs. "Go on."

I dragged myself up the stairs, considering my options. Wear dinosaur pajamas to school? Kyle would love that. Convince Mom I was too sick to go to school until my jeans were dry? No chance. Tell her about my dinosaurs? She'd never believe me because they were just models to her. I'd only be in more trouble.

Could I ask her to go into my closet? But she'd see the mess and never let me keep my door closed. Then the beast would tear apart the whole house when Mom and Dad weren't looking. Maybe I could just throw myself out my window and break a leg. Then I wouldn't have to go to school. But I'd have to stay home with the beast. I finally decided I had to go into the closet.

I shut my door, turned on the radio and packed Stegy away inside two boxes so he'd be totally out of reach of the beast. I pulled on an old sweatshirt and tugged on a pillowcase like a helmet, the pillow still inside.

I unpacked one of my plastic boxes to drop on top of him. I pushed my dresser to one side and picked up the plastic container. Taking a deep breath, I pulled open the closet doors, ready to drop the box on top of the beast.

But he was too fast. In a flash, he was out of the closet, racing around the room, hissing and clawing. He must have smelled Stegy, because he attacked Stegy's boxes with a roar. I chased after him with my container, dropping it down on him, but I only caught one leg. He yanked it free and turned on me.

The pillow protected my head, but he scratched my cheeks, clawed holes in my sweatshirt and tore right through my pajama pants. Finally I trapped him with the plastic container while he was trying to shred my feet. I stood with one foot on top of the box, ignoring his shrieks, while I pulled jeans and clean pajamas out of my closet. Then I scooped out all the plastic lids and bits of rotting meat, and pushed the plastic box inside the closet. But how was I going to get it off him and still keep him trapped?

Maybe I could just leave him in it. I sighed—it really was too small. I wasn't that mean, even if he was. I pulled the closet doors almost shut; then I used a ruler to flip over the box. While the beast attacked the doors, I pushed them shut and dragged my dresser back into place.

Finally I sat on my bed with a thump and checked out the damage. Sweatshirt and pajama bottoms— trashed. Stegy safe. Room stinking of meat. I opened the window and bagged up the garbage.

Me? I snuck into the bathroom to check. Scratched face, arms, chest and legs. Bleeding feet. I scrubbed and sprayed all the scrapes. We were almost out of antiseptic spray; I'd have to make up a story for Mom. Luckily she was drowning in tax returns, so she might not pay attention.

I pulled on clean jeans and a long-sleeved shirt, even though it was nice out. Nothing else would cover my scratches. Then I made up a story at breakfast.

"What happened to your face?" Mom asked, turning my head to examine my cheek.

"I tripped and fell" I said. "I tore my dinosaur pajama pants too. I know you're busy right now—you don't have to try to fix them. I have others."

She looked at me, puzzled. I was usually fanatical about anything with dinosaurs on them. But she really was busy, so she let it go and went back to making coffee.

"I cleaned the scrape," I said. "We're almost out of antiseptic spray."

"I'll put it on the shopping list," she said, jotting it on the list on the fridge. Then she stood, pencil in hand, looking around the kitchen.

"Coffee," I said. "You were making coffee."

She smiled. "Thanks, hon. I'm a little distracted these days."

"I know," I said. "Tax season."

But I guess she wasn't as distracted as I thought. After dinner I heard her talking to Dad. "I called Lucas's teacher today, Miss Dubois. I'm worried he doesn't have any friends. Miss Dubois says he's a nice boy who gets along well with most of the kids."

Dad said, "He's just quiet. Don't worry so much."

"But I do worry. And Miss Dubois agreed to help. She said there's another boy in the class who doesn't seem to have any close friends, and she'll try to encourage them to work together."

Kyle, I thought as I listened from the stairs. He was the only other kid in the class who didn't have friends. Everyone was afraid of him, afraid they'd become his next target. I couldn't cope with Kyle *and* the beast. And since I couldn't do anything about Kyle, I was going to have to get rid of the beast. Somehow.

CHAPTER 5

Get Rid of It!

Saturday morning I tackled the beast. Literally. I waited until Mom was working in her office and Dad was vacuuming. I found a cardboard box in the garage and borrowed a roll of packing tape. I pushed Stegy into his box, shut the window and the door, and turned on the radio, loud. Then I dressed in my torn sweatshirt and pulled my ragged pajama pants over my jeans, strapped on my bike helmet and pulled on Mom's leather gardening gloves.

I tried to pretend I was a brave gladiator, but I didn't feel very brave when I pushed the dresser away from the closet doors. Mostly I felt queasy.

I squared my shoulders, picked up my box and tried to feel tough. Slowly, I eased open the closet doors a crack. Maybe the beast was sleeping and I could trap him easily.

But suddenly he was smashing against the doors, screeching and clawing. When I didn't open them any further, he roared with fury and launched himself at the doors again. He pulled back and threw himself at them, over and over. The rhythm gave me an idea. I set the box right by the opening and waited. He smashed against the doors, drew back and smashed again. When he drew back once more, I opened the doors so that instead of hitting the doors, he flew past them, right into the box. Yes!

I flipped over one flap, then turned the box upright and scrambled for the others. He clawed past them. I pushed him in and pulled down another flap. He ripped at my gloves but the leather protected me. He tried again, higher this time, and tore a gouge down my wrist. I stifled a scream, shook him off and pushed him back down again. Then I held all four flaps in place with one hand while I groped for the packing tape with the other.

I tugged off a leather glove with my teeth and held the tape between my knees while I tried to find the end. My other hand was fighting to keep the beast in the box. Finally I stood, with one foot on the top of the box, so I could get both hands on the roll of tape. I ran my fingers around and around the roll until I found an end. I picked it loose and unrolled a length of tape. Kneeling, I started strapping up the box. The beast sank his teeth into my bare fingers as they passed by the opening between the flaps. I poked him in the eye with my other hand, and he let go with a shriek. Quickly I taped up the opening. Then I wrapped tape around and around the box.

Feeling clever, I wiped the blood off my hands with a tissue and snuck down the stairs with the shrieking box. I carried it out to the garbage bin outside the back fence and dropped it into a can with a thump. You can go live at the dump, I thought. There'll be lots of food and it'll be far from me! I banged down the lid on the can, dropped down the lid of the bin and bounced back to the house. I had done it. I was free of the beast!

I hung out in my room all morning. I cleaned up the closet floor, opened the windows and let Stegy wander. He wouldn't go near the closet, but he loved exploring the rest of the room. After lunch, I took him out to the yard. He feasted on dandelion greens, tiny shoots of chives and long crabgrass spears. Together we explored the garden, finding every plant that was pushing its way out of the dirt. We had a great day.

After dinner, Mom took out the garbage and came back fuming. "A dog has torn apart the garbage bags and strewn garbage all over the place. And I have nineteen tax returns to finish!"

Dad looked over his shoulder at her, his hands in the kitchen sink, washing dishes. "Lucas can do it. Take a big green garbage bag, will you? Just bag up everything. You can wear gardening gloves if you want. Then make sure the bin lid is down."

I stood immobile in the middle of the kitchen. I was pretty sure no dog had dug around in our garbage bin.

"Lucas?" Mom shook me. "Go ahead. You're old enough to help with gross chores."

I looked up at her with huge eyes. "But Mooom—"

"What? Dad and I are both busy. You don't think you can do it?" She raised her eyebrows, making it perfectly clear what the right answer was.

"No, I'll do it," I said, my voice weak.

Dad smiled as he turned back to the dishes; he didn't say anything to save me.

I armed myself again—with a torn sweatshirt, a garbage bag and leather gloves. I didn't think they'd understand the bike helmet; I'd just have to hope the beast was long gone.

He was. I could see where he had chewed open the cardboard box. And I could see, from how far the garbage was flung across the alley, that he was really, really angry. But I couldn't figure out how he had opened the garbage bin lid. Was he really that strong?

That thought left me shaking as I hurried to pick up the garbage. I wanted to get back inside before he knew I was out here. I was almost done when Kyle walked by.

"Ah, the garbage boy!" he said with a nasty smirk. "Were you a bad boy? Parents make you do the nasty job?"

I just ignored him and leaned down to pick up the last crumpled paper. Kyle was stepping closer when he heard our back door shut. He turned and walked away, muttering, "About time, too. Spoiled brat!"

He thought I was spoiled? I didn't have a computer or a TV in my room, not like lots of kids. I wasn't spoiled! I glared as he walked down the alley, cool in his oversized sweatshirt. At least I didn't wear the same shirt every day!

Dad came out just as I was finishing.

"Nice job," he said as he lifted the full garbage bag into the bin for me. As we walked back through the yard, he stopped and leaned down near the raspberry canes. He reached out an arm and stood up with the beast in his hand. "You must have left this outside when you were playing earlier. Don't leave it out in the rain—it's your best model yet."

I stared at the beast in horror. I did not want him back! But Dad would never understand. Slowly I took him from Dad. Then, just as slowly, an idea formed.

"Hey, Dad, I'm having trouble with my math. Could you come up and help me?" Maybe if he came up to my room with me, I could get the beast into my closet while he was still motionless.

"Sure," Dad said, patting my shoulder. "Always glad to help with math."

That was the problem. Dad was an engineer and Mom was an accountant, so they didn't understand a son who just didn't like math. And I didn't want Dad any more involved than he had to be. But maybe this would be worth it.

I left the beast in the kitchen while Dad finished up the dishes and I put away the gloves and washed my hands. Then I picked up the beast, and Dad and

I walked upstairs to my room. The beast was perfectly still, but I swear he was glaring at me while I carried him up the stairs.

As soon as I was in my room, I put him down in the closet and shut the doors. He glared at me as his room went dark.

Dad sat on the bed and said, "So what's the problem with math?" He glanced around my room—looking for math homework, I guess.

Of course I didn't have any this weekend. So I made the ultimate sacrifice. "I'm just so slow with my times tables," I said, hoping he'd be too busy to care. No such luck. I should have asked Mom.

"Let's get out the flash cards and I'll help you practice."

"I'm not sure where they are," I said, hoping to get out of it.

Dad smiled. "Take a look, and if you can't find them, we'll make some more."

I sighed and dug through my school stuff until I found the flash cards. I was awful. I'm always bad at times tables, but I was too worried about what to do with the beast to remember even the ones I usually knew.

"Wow, you really are struggling with this," Dad said. "We'll have to make time to practice every night."

No no no no no!!! Not Kyle and the beast and math flash cards!!!! When Dad left, I slowly pushed the chest of drawers back in front of the closet and sagged against it. What was I going to do?

CHAPTER 6

Dinosaurs at the Zoo

Sunday I came up with a new plan. On Monday my class was going to the zoo, and I decided to take the beast with me. I figured that once we were around other people, he'd be quiet. I found my old red little-kid's backpack in the garage. I'd stuff him in it and put it inside my own backpack. Then I'd just leave him somewhere at the zoo. He could live wild there. If anyone came near him, he would look like a model, so he couldn't hurt anyone. I hoped.

Monday, Dad set out some chunks of beef to thaw for stew. When no one was looking I swiped three. They were frozen solid, so I popped them into the micro-wave on defrost for a minute before I slid them into a Baggie. I'd given the beast water but no food, so he'd be extra hungry.

One last time, I shoved aside my dresser. I laid my red backpack on the floor, stuffed in a layer of newspapers to line the bottom and dumped the raw meat inside. The beast smelled it, even through the shut closet doors, and started to roar.

I opened the doors a crack and pushed the top of the backpack inside. I tried to waft some of the smell of raw meat to the beast, but he just flung himself at the gap between the doors and clawed, trying to pry the doors apart. So I tugged the bag wide, opened the closet doors and let him out.

He hurled himself out of the closet. I jumped back and grabbed the duvet off my bed to protect myself. But he didn't go far before he started sniffing. He turned to the backpack lying near the closet and burrowed into it, searching for the meat. I held it open for him, and once he was eating, I closed the bag around him and zipped it up.

I could hear him devouring the meat while I finished getting ready. First I pulled some clean pants out of the closet, cleaned up the closet floor, fed Stegy and pulled out my own backpack. Then I emptied all the junk out of the bottom of my pack and stuffed in the beast in his bag. I slid my notebook and pencil case down beside the red backpack and set my lunch on top. With that, I was ready to go. At least I hoped I was.

My class met in front of the school. It was sunny but cool, with a sharp spring wind. Kyle stood to one side, arms crossed, looking bored but tough at the same time. No one went near him. No one came near me, either. When the yellow school bus pulled up, we all raced to it. Miss Dubois stood by the steps and ticked off our names on her clipboard as we climbed on.

Kyle hung back; he wasn't going to push through the crowd. But he'd get the back seat anyway. No one wanted to argue with him about that.

I asked Miss Dubois if I could sit with her. That way I'd be at the front of the bus, far from Kyle. She looked at me, surprised, until I said I wanted to tell her more about my dinosaur models. Then she smiled and patted my head. Sweet boy, her smile said. I flushed but stuck with it. Having her think I was sweet was better than sitting near Kyle.

I sat in the front seat by the door. Kyle sneered as he walked past me. When Miss Dubois had all the kids and volunteer parents seated and counted, she sat beside me with a sigh, clipboard on her lap. She wore black glasses, and her straight brown hair was pulled back in a ponytail. When Mom first met her, she was shocked at how young Miss Dubois was. She seems pretty old to me, but she's nice.

We talked a little about making dinosaur models, but mostly she stayed busy keeping everyone quiet. I could hear Kyle bugging other kids, but he didn't bother me. I was in the only safe spot on the bus.

My stomach flipped every time the bus bumped over a pothole and I slid into my backpack, but the beast stayed quiet. I sat twitching with nervousness, praying my plan would work, terrified it wouldn't.

When I got really fidgety, Miss Dubois turned to me and smiled. "Excited?" she asked.

I smiled weakly. You have no idea, I thought. What I said was, "Oh, yeah. I love the zoo. Especially the dinosaur park. Are we going there?"

"We'll have some time after lunch to divide into groups and go to our favorite parts of the zoo," she said. "You'll get there."

I grinned. Yes! That's where I'd leave the beast!

When we got to the zoo, everyone gathered around the parent volunteers. Some kids stood near their parents, and their friends crowded close so they'd be in the same group. The rest of us stood around, looking awkward.

I could see Miss Dubois glancing from Kyle to me to the parents. I could tell she was planning on pairing us up. I took a quick look over the groups. Then I walked over to Jenny, who was standing alone with her mom. "Can I be in your group?" I asked.

Jenny's really small. She looked up at me, her blond hair swinging back from her face. "Sure," she said, looking surprised.

No one wanted to be with Jenny because she was the bossiest girl in the whole school. Kyle couldn't stand her. He didn't dare bug her, and he'd do anything to stay out of her group.

Miss Dubois put a couple of other kids with us, quiet kids who wouldn't argue with Jenny. She bossed us all day. But I didn't care. Being bossed by Jenny was infinitely better than being bullied by Kyle.

Our day started with a lecture on animal care. Then we watched the elephants having a bath. We finished the morning making treats for the gorillas in the loft above the otters. Miss Dubois pulled out a bag filled with toilet paper tubes we'd collected. I grabbed a tube and sat down near the end of a long table. I checked on the beast; he was still quiet, still motionless. I breathed a sigh of relief. Then I looked up, straight at Kyle staring at me from across the table.

We blocked one end of our tubes with cardboard and edible glue and filled the tubes with popcorn and spices. I couldn't figure out why gorillas would like all those strong spices, but I wasn't about to ask. I just kept my head down and worked, trying to ignore Kyle.

He didn't like being ignored. "Hey, Lucas," he whispered as soon as Miss Dubois was at another table. "Maybe we can feed you to the gorillas. Except they'd probably throw you back." Then he paused, made a face and said, in a squeaky voice, "Eww—red·hair? I'm not eating that!"

While the kids around us laughed, I stuffed my tube full and covered the top end with cardboard. Don't react, just don't react, I repeated to myself.

We ate lunch in the loft. I sat on the floor against the wall, leaving Kyle at the table cracking jokes. When I pulled out my lunch bag, I could feel the beast shifting around.

After lunch, we took our gorilla snacks to the gorilla enclosure. It's huge, with lots of places for the gorillas to climb and play, and walkways for people to watch from. We took turns tossing the snacks off the top pathway down to the gorillas. Then we raced down the steps to watch the gorillas fight over them. One smart girl gorilla found two snacks, but some older boys stole them from her. Just like Kyle, I thought. Bullies everywhere.

Finally we had a free hour to explore our favorite spots. I joined the kids going to the dinosaur park.

Jenny wanted to see the kangaroos, but Kyle joined my group. Miss Dubois looked pleased; she was determined for us to be friends.

Some people think it's weird to have a dinosaur park in a zoo. After all, a zoo is supposed to be about live animals. But it's my favorite part. It's landscaped to look like southern Alberta did when dinosaurs lived here, with primitive plants and weird rock formations. All through it, dinosaur models graze and wade in the pond and loom over the pathways. It's the coolest place in Calgary and my second-favorite place in the world. My absolute number one favorite is the dinosaur museum in Drumheller—the Royal Tyrrell Museum of Paleontology. But we only get out there a few times a year, so the zoo was a close second.

Our volunteer said we could go anywhere we wanted as long as we stayed in the dinosaur park and met her in exactly one hour. That worked for me.

I stood in the center of the dinosaur park, on a high spot overlooking the small lake. A few last patches of snow gleamed white in shady spots; green sprouted up in the gardens. I had trouble imagining dinosaurs surrounded by snow and surviving on tiny spring shoots. But it was the best time to see the dinosaurs, as they loomed over the bare gardens. By late summer, they would be hidden in the plants.

Now if I could just stay away from Kyle and get rid of the beast, my day would be perfect. I looked around for someplace to leave the bag. There's a sort of cave I thought would be a good spot to hide it. I pretended I really was in a land of dinosaurs as I followed the path around the volcano and slipped into the cave. I waited until I was alone. Then I opened my backpack. Checking over my shoulder to make sure no one was coming, I pulled the little red backpack out of my back-pack and set it on a ledge. The beast was quiet—still gorged on meat, I hoped. I shoved the bag far back into a corner, gave it a little pat goodbye and slipped out.

The rest of the hour in the dinosaur park was so much fun. Whenever I spotted Kyle, I avoided him like he was a tyrannosaurus and I was a smaller and much more clever dinosaur. I checked out every dino-saur in the park and imagined what I would create if I was hired to make more. When it was finally time to leave, we gathered just inside the gates while Miss Dubois checked us off on her clipboard. I stood lis-tening to Jenny insisting that we stay together and not climb on the rocks.

I was ignoring her, imagining making more dinosaur models, when Kyle showed up. He was carrying my little red backpack. He held it like it was his, like he was trying not to draw attention to it, but Miss Dubois noticed right away. I drew back into the crowd of kids, hoping she wouldn't see me.

"What's that, Kyle?" she asked.

"Huh?" he said, trying to look casual. But she was already reaching for it.

"Oh, uh, I found this," he said. "In the dinosaur park. I don't know who it belongs to."

My heart stopped as she opened the bag. What if the beast attacked? I imagined him leaping up, claws ripping at her cheek. But when she lifted him out, he was just a model.

"This looks like one of Lucas's," she said. She looked up and scanned the group of kids until she spotted me. "Lucas," she called.

I sighed and stepped forward.

"Is this yours?" she asked.

I was about to deny it when Kyle smiled a fake smile and handed me the bag. I nodded and took the beast from Miss Dubois. "I must have put it down and forgotten it," I said.

"Thanks, Kyle," Miss Dubois said. "Why don't you two sit together on the way home?"

I looked at her, horrified. Then Jenny, of all people, saved me. "He's going to sit with me," she said. "I want to learn how he makes dinosaurs."

She glared at Kyle, daring him to complain. With her mom and Miss Dubois there, he couldn't say a thing. But he grinned at me as he walked away. *I couldn't do anything worse to you than a bus ride with Jenny*, his grin said.

As Kyle strode off in front of the class and Jenny bugged everyone to keep up, I slipped off to a garbage can and dropped the little red backpack into it.

"Goodbye, you monster," I said as I walked away.

I had to run to catch up with the others. Jenny grabbed my arm and hurried me to the rest of the class, scolding all the way. I didn't care. Inside I was laughing.

CHAPTER 7

The Cat Came Back

The next days were great. The weather was great, the blue sky was great, even the greening-up grass was great. I was free! Kyle was horrible, but I just rubbed the scars on my arms and was thankful I only had Kyle to deal with.

Dad kept me practicing times tables, but since the beast was gone I could remember things again. He was so pleased with my improvement that he stopped insisting we practice every night.

For weeks, life was great, until one night near the end of April. Mom was frantic, with only days left to finish her clients' tax returns. Dad was tired of doing all the cooking and cleaning, so he'd ordered Indian take-out.

I had just served myself a big pile of palao rice and butter chicken when we heard screeching in the garden. We turned to the French doors leading out to the back-yard. All we could see was a flurry of movement and then a fluttering of feathers on the deck.

"An owl must have caught a bird," my dad said, turning back to his supper.

But I wasn't so sure. Most of the feathers were black and white and small, like from a chickadee, but one larger feather was soft brown, a lot like the feathers I'd bought for making the beast. I looked around the yard and glimpsed something slipping into the bushes. It didn't look much like an owl.

Suddenly I felt so sick I couldn't swallow my mouthful of butter chicken. I ran to the bathroom and spat it into the toilet. I rinsed out my mouth and washed my hands while I talked to myself in the mirror. "What if the beast is back? How could he be? Not from the zoo—that's too far!"

All through dinner I was hyperalert, twitching at every sound from outside. All I could eat was rice and naan bread; just the thought of eating anything else turned my stomach.

After I carried my plate to the kitchen counter, I walked back to the French doors and stared outside.

I couldn't see a thing out of place in the backyard, except the sprinkling of feathers on the deck. But that was enough. A bird had died, and I was pretty sure it was because of me.

Then I heard a yowl. It came from the front of the house, not the backyard. I ran to the living room window, searching for what had made the sound. There, in the far corner of the yard, near the sidewalk, was Mr. Garner's ginger cat, back arched, hissing at a bush. She clawed at something and then leapt forward. My heart surged; maybe she was hunting the beast! Maybe she could stop him! She and the beast rolled out of the bush, clawing and scratching at each other. She was bigger; surely she would win. But then, with a terrible yowl, she jumped free and raced across the road.

The beast sat back, and I swear he smirked. He was back! How did he get here from the zoo? Why was he alive to other animals, but not for all humans?

I felt like I was living in some horror version of that song "The Cat Came Back." When I was little I'd sing the chorus with Dad. We'd end all slow and sad, "But the cat came back, he just wouldn't stay away."

It was a favorite of my dad's, and I used to like it. Not anymore. How had he found me? What was I going to do?

When the beast disappeared into the bushes, I yelled for Dad. "There's something in the front yard. It scared Mr. Garner's cat. Come look with me?"

He walked out of the kitchen, wiping his hands on a towel. He stood beside me, peering out the window. "I don't see anything."

"There, by the bushes," I said, pointing. "Mr. Garner's cat attacked something. Then he ran away, yowling."

"Let's have a look, then," Dad said as he put down the towel.

We slipped on our shoes and walked into the front yard. I held back while Dad walked straight to the far corner of the yard. He laughed and leaned down. When he stood he was holding the beast.

"Do you think this scared her?" he asked, still laughing. "Maybe you shouldn't make them so realistic," he said as he handed the beast to me.

Maybe not, I thought, stifling an hysterical laugh.

As we walked back into the house, I said, "Come up to my room? I'd like to talk about what I might make next."

Dad shook his head. "Sorry, Lucas, but I have to finish in the kitchen. Your mom's already back at work."

I sighed and turned to go upstairs. Then I changed my mind and followed Dad into the kitchen, grabbed a cookie and headed upstairs.

As soon as I was out of Dad's sight, the beast came to life. He tightened his claws on my hand. Then he turned and glared at me. I swear he looked just like Kyle planning something nasty.

Hesitantly, I held out the cookie. I'd only ever seen him eat meat, but maybe he liked gingersnaps. The beast sniffed at it, snatched it up and ate it, cookie bits flying. He was like the Cookie Monster gone to the dark side. I shuddered as I scrambled up the stairs and into my room. He just stared at me while he devoured his cookie.

I dashed to my closet, but the doors were closed. I set the beast down on my bed with the cookie, hip-checked the bedroom door shut and nudged Stegy into his box with my foot. I opened the closet doors and grabbed a plastic box from under the table. I dumped out all the craft supplies, buttons rolling everywhere, and dropped the box over the beast. He shrieked, but I ignored him. I slid a sheet of cardboard underneath the box and carried the whole thing to the closet. I set it on the closet floor and shut the doors, my hands shaking.

Once the beast was safely in the closet, with my dresser pushed in front of the doors again, I knelt by Stegy's box and pulled him out. He was quivering; so was I. I petted him. Then I set him down so he could wander. I sat in a daze, not having a clue what to do. But I had to do something! I couldn't live like this.

Stegy's box, the box the dinosaur-making potion came in, lay beside me on the floor. I glared at it, hating the potion that started all this.

Then I started to think. Maybe if I reread the instructions I could figure out what to do. I jumped up, excited. Maybe my answer lay on that little bit of paper! But where was it?

I prayed while I searched: please, please, please let there be an answer on the paper. I finally found the test tube in its Baggie at the bottom of a plastic box, surrounded by loose buttons and escaped googly eyes.

I grabbed the Baggie and pulled out the paper with shaking hands. I almost couldn't bear to read it—what if it didn't help? Slowly I unfolded it, closed my eyes for a moment, and read:

Make A Dinosaur Come To Life

Mix the solution with your papier-mâché goop (glue or flour paste) and make a papier-mâché dinosaur. There is enough for three small projects or one large. You will be astounded at how lifelike your dinosaur will become for you. But be warned: what you create is yours for life unless it is stolen from you.
www.howweirdcanyouget.com

My heart dropped to the floor. No one would ever steal it! I was stuck with it for life!

I imagined years of torn sweatshirts and dirty jeans and a stinky closet. I imagined Mom more and more mad at me. And if I tried to tell my parents, they'd never believe me, because he was never alive when they saw him! I sat at my desk, slumped in misery.

I finally moved when I heard whistling. I looked out my window and saw Kyle walking by. He stopped right in front of my house but was staring across the street. What was he looking at? He glanced at my house, turned back and lobbed a rock at Mr. Garner's cat.

What a creep! *He'd* steal the beast, if he could. He was mean enough! I didn't think he'd break into my house, but if he could steal it at school, say, he would. I just bet he would!

Then I thought about it. Kyle would steal the beast. Could I leave him somewhere, accidentally? Someplace Kyle would walk by? Then the beast would be gone from my life and—bonus—Kyle would be stuck with him! How cool was that? But how could I do it?

CHAPTER 8

To Catch a Thief

I planned all night while Mom and Dad thought I was sleeping. As soon as it was light, I jumped out of bed and set to work. First, I snuck downstairs for lettuce, a carrot and sliced roast beef. I'd convinced my parents I wanted roast beef for lunch every day, so I had a regular supply for the beast. I dug an old leather bag Mom never used out of the hall cupboard.

I fed Stegy and then let him wander while I made my bed and packed up my backpack. I put on a long-sleeved T-shirt and jeans, with my torn sweatshirt over top. If I sent any more torn clothes to the laundry, Mom was sure to notice, even in tax season.

Then I pushed Stegy into his box and set Mom's leather bag by the closet doors with a slice of roast beef in the bottom and some more nearby. I pulled on my bike helmet and leather gloves. Then, and only then, I pushed aside my dresser and opened the closet doors just a crack. I slipped a piece of meat in and dropped it to the floor. The beast pounced before I heard the meat land.

While he was eating, I yanked open the closet doors and dropped the bag over his head. He shrieked and fought while I tried to stuff him deep into the bag; I wished I'd remembered to turn on my radio.

"Lucas?" Mom called from down the hall.

"Just practicing dinosaur calls," I yelled back.

"A little quieter, please. It sounds like something's dying in there."

"I'll try," I said, struggling to push the beast further into the bag. He sank his teeth into my thumb and clung. I pushed him down with that hand, while his teeth were busy, and grabbed him with my other hand through the bag and squeezed. He let go of my thumb with a shriek.

"Lucas!"

I quickly tied up the bag. "Sorry!"

The beast finally settled down to gorge on the roast beef I'd left in the bottom of the bag.

I looked at the blood oozing from the row of holes on my thumb. The thought of the roast beef on the beast's teeth ground into my flesh was disgusting. I scrubbed my thumb, sprayed it and wrapped it in a bandage.

Only then, when the beast couldn't do any more damage, did I change into my black tyrannosaurus rex T-shirt, the one with the white skull across the front and a dark gray head rising up behind it. I wanted to get Kyle's attention first thing.

It worked. Kyle stopped me in the schoolyard. "Trying to look tough, Lark?" he said. "No more feather-brain dinosaurs?"

I stared back at him, trying not to smile. I'd teach him about feather-brain dinosaurs!

All day Kyle glared at anyone who came near me. I didn't care. Soon I'd be free of the beast, and Kyle would be stuck with him! I just knew my plan would work.

I made sure he saw what was in the bag. At lunch-time I lifted out the beast while Kyle was grabbing his lunch. He pretended not to be interested, but I could feel him watching me put the beast back into the bag.

After school I loaded up my backpack with all the junk from my desk: dinosaur drawings, books, work

I'd finished and didn't need at school anymore. Soon my backpack was stuffed. I slung it on my back, carried the leather bag with the beast in my left hand and cradled a pile of dinosaur books in my right arm.

I made sure Kyle was around when I left the school; I kept glancing back at him, as if I was afraid and didn't want him to follow me. Of course he did. Which was perfect, absolutely perfect.

I walked around the school, and just before the corner, where there are lots of bushes growing under the windows, I accidentally-on-purpose tripped, flinging my books into the air and giving the leather bag a toss into the bushes. I scrambled around on my knees, picking up my books, glancing back at Kyle, who stood and watched with a huge grin on his face. Then I limped around the corner, clinging to my stack of books.

As soon as I was out of sight, I stopped and leaned against the school wall, panting. Then I peeked around the corner. I laughed at Kyle's blue-jeaned bum sticking out from the bushes. He straightened up with the leather bag in his hand and a smile on his face. I ducked back as he glanced around to make sure no one had seen him. He headed home, whistling, and I walked off in the other direction, whistling just like Kyle.

The next day Kyle came to school looking haunted. His face was pale, except for dark smudges under his eyes. He had scratches down his cheek, a gouge on his neck his collar couldn't quite hide and bandages on his hands. His arms were hidden by his long-sleeved shirt.

And he twitched. He jumped at every little sound.

I started explaining dinosaur cries to Jacob just so I could let out a screech like the beast's. Kyle leapt from his chair, hands up to guard his face, looking frantically around the room. I tried to look innocent when he glared at me, but I had trouble hiding my grin.

The next days were awesome. Kyle wore pants and long-sleeved shirts every day, even though it was spring and warm outside. Everyone else wore T-shirts and shorts, except me, of course. But I didn't care. My scratches were healing; I knew he was getting new ones every day.

His hands were a mess. Miss Dubois started to fuss over him, but he told her something about climbing trees, and she believed him enough to drop it. I just shook my head. Why didn't he wear leather gloves? And lock the beast in his closet? I almost felt sorry for him. Almost.

The best thing was that Kyle stopped bugging me. He'd sit at his desk and glower, but as long as he sat, he didn't scare the other kids and they started to talk to me. Every day I wore a different dinosaur T-shirt, and every day they were admired. I brought books, too—my favorite books on dinosaurs—and at lunchtime I taught Jacob and Ian how to draw dinosaurs. They needed to pay more attention to how dinosaurs really looked, so I pulled out the books and we talked about skeletons while we drew.

And sometimes I just sat back and enjoyed it. I had read somewhere that revenge is sweet, but I didn't really understand, until now. It's true. Revenge is very, very sweet.

Then I learned that revenge is tricky too.

We had an early May heat wave, and everyone dug out their summer clothes and came to school in shorts and sandals. Everyone except Kyle and me. Together, we sweated in our long-sleeved shirts and jeans. Neither of us wore sandals. I had nasty scratches on my feet that were healing really slowly, and I guessed that Kyle had fresh ones.

While I was sweating and feeling cranky from the heat, I felt a twinge of sympathy for Kyle. But it didn't last long. He deserved it!

Kyle looked worse every day. He just didn't seem to be learning how to protect himself from the beast. Every day he had new gouges on his hands and scratches on his face. Why wasn't he keeping the beast locked away? And why didn't he wear gloves? What was his problem?

Kyle grew more and more pale, the shadows under his eyes darker and darker. Every day he had new scratches. Miss Dubois became really concerned, but Kyle made up a story for her.

"I want to be a tree-climbing champion," he said, trying to smile at her. "So I climb every day. Sometimes I get scratched a bit, but I haven't fallen yet!" He said that with a flash of the old Kyle, and she smiled.

"Just be careful, okay?" she said. "I don't want you in here with a broken leg."

I tried to convince myself that I didn't care, that he deserved it, but that got harder and harder. I started to hear the beast in my dreams, screaming and scratching, but at Kyle instead of me. I'd pull my pillow tight against my head, trying to silence the cries, but they echoed in my sleep.

And then one morning when we were playing basketball, Kyle's sleeve fell back and I saw his left arm. It was covered in a maze of red lines, some shallow, some deep. It looked like he hadn't cleaned them properly—they were raised and red, like the welts Mom gets from pruning. I could hardly see any normal skin between the scratches. He yanked his sleeve down and glanced around to see if anyone had noticed. I just knelt to tie my shoelace.

But all day I felt like the most horrible person in the world. I had done this to him. I had set him up to steal the beast. I knew how to handle the beast, but I hadn't told Kyle. I'd let him get attacked day after day after day.

All his meanness suddenly seemed like nothing compared to mine.

CHAPTER 9

Parley

At recess, I waited outside for Kyle. When he came out of the school, I knew he didn't want to talk to me. I think he was too miserable to want to talk to anyone. But I stood in his path and said, "You need to come to my house. I have something to show you."

Kyle was immediately suspicious. "Why would I want to go to your house?"

I yanked up his sleeve, exposing the long scratches up his arm. "That's why."

He flushed and tugged down his sleeve. "That's none of your business," he said, his voice angry.

I rolled up my right sleeve. When he saw the partially healed scratches up my arm, his mouth fell open and he stared at me in silence.

I pushed his chin up to close his mouth and said, "My place, after school."

He gulped and nodded.

I walked away shaking—why did I do that? I really didn't want to have anything to do with Kyle or the beast. Maybe he won't come, I thought, and that was my only comfort all afternoon.

But Kyle was waiting for me after school. We walked to my house without talking. It was another great day, sunny and clear. But I stared down all the way home, wondering how I was going to explain this to Kyle, how he'd react, what he'd do when he realized I'd set him up.

Mom was in the front yard raking. When she saw us, she leaned on her rake and smiled.

"Hi, Mom," I said. "Is it okay if Kyle comes over? We need to work on a project."

"Of course you can have a friend over," Mom said, trying to control her grin. "If I'd known, I'd have baked some cookies." She reached down to pick up a green garbage bag. "Make sure you guys have a snack before you head upstairs."

She knelt by a pile of dead grass and called out to us as we walked away. "Kyle, does your mom know where you are?"

Kyle flushed and then muttered, "I'll tell my dad."

As we walked into the kitchen, I pointed at the phone. "Need to use the phone?"

Kyle looked blank.

"To call your dad?"

"Oh, I'll call him later."

I shrugged and opened the fridge. "What do you want to eat?"

This time Kyle shrugged. "Anything's fine."

"No, really, would you like crackers? Fruit? Cookies?"

"Whatever," he said, staring at the floor.

I rolled my eyes, grabbed a bag of chocolate chip cookies and poured two glasses of milk.

When I sat at the table, Kyle crossed his arms and glared at me. "Clarke, I didn't come here for milk and cookies," he said.

I pushed a glass toward him. "Yeah, I know, but I'm really hungry and Mom won't let me take food up to my room. So eat. Then we'll go upstairs. I have something to show you."

Kyle sat with a sigh, gulped down the milk and devoured seven cookies. While he ate, he looked around the kitchen. Mom had just cleaned it, in her annual post-tax-season cleaning binge. "Nice place," said Kyle. I wasn't sure what I heard in his voice; it almost sounded like envy.

"Yeah, it's okay," I said, shrugging. It seemed pretty regular to me.

"Is your mom home all the time?" he asked.

"She works from home," I said. "She's an accountant. She just finished tax season, so now she has time for other things."

Kyle stuffed in another cookie. "And your dad?"

"He's an engineer. He works downtown. What does your dad do?"

"He's in construction," Kyle said as he jumped up. "Come on, Clarke, we've eaten half the bag of cookies. Let's get on with it."

I could have sat eating cookies all afternoon. Not because I love cookies that much—well, I do—but to avoid telling Kyle what I'd done. My body felt like lead as I dragged it up the stairs.

We dropped our backpacks inside my bedroom door and I turned on the radio. I figured once I told

Kyle what I'd done, it would get as noisy in here as when the beast was loose.

I wasn't sure how to explain all this to Kyle. I finally decided to start by telling him about howweirdcan youget.com.

After I described it, Kyle just said, "You found it on your mom's computer? You don't have your own?"

"No, I don't have my own," I said. "You act like I'm some kind of spoiled brat. But look around: no computer, no TV, no CD player."

Kyle looked around my room, his face still. My room was pretty clean for once: bed made, only a few clothes on the floor, shelves loaded with books, dinosaur models hanging around the room. He just shook his head and shrugged. Then he sat on my bed. "So you found a website. Big deal."

"Yeah, well, it turned out to be a really big deal." I dug around until I found the test tube of liquid and the paper explaining how to use it.

Kyle tipped the test tube back and forth; then he shook it. My fingers twitched, worried he'd break it. But he handed it back and read the paper. Then he started to laugh. "Oh, come on. You believed this!?"

"No," I snapped. "I didn't believe it." I started to look for Stegy, checking behind my boxes and then dropping to my hands and knees to search under the bed. I had to lie flat to reach him. I squirmed out with him in my right hand.

"I just made a dinosaur, using that book I did a book report on. But I poured in a little of this stuff to see what would happen."

Kyle yawned. "Uh-huh?"

"Well," I said. "Stegy here, he, uh…" I stopped—this was really hard to say. "He, uh, he came to life."

"Sure, just like Frosty the Snowman," Kyle said, laughing. But his laughter sounded a little forced.

I grabbed his arm, pulled up his sleeve and then pushed up both of mine. "No," I said, my voice full of anger, "not even a little like Frosty the Snowman!"

That shut him up. He looked from my arms to his and then at Stegy. Slowly he pushed his sleeve down. "But he's not moving."

"Yeah, that's because you didn't steal him," I snapped. "I made him, so he's only real for me. Unless someone steals him."

Kyle sat in silence. Then he cleared his throat. "So you made another?"

"Yeah," I said. "Stegy's so great, I wanted another one."

"He's great?"

"Oh, yeah," I said. "He's a stegosaurus. They're herbivores, so he'll fight to protect himself, but he doesn't attack or anything. He's a really nice pet."

Kyle sat quietly, holding Stegy, turning him over and over. "And the other one?"

"It's a sinornithosaurus, a carnivore, a predator—and he's ferocious."

Kyle rubbed his arms. "No kidding." He picked up the paper and read it again. "'Yours for life unless it is stolen.' So that monster is alive for me instead of being a model like Stegy is..."

"Well, Stegy's alive for me..."

"Yeah, but a model for me. That sin-no-nor-tho..."

"I just call him the beast," I said.

Kyle nodded. "The beast is alive for me because I stole him from you?"

I nodded.

Kyle closed his eyes and leaned forward. "Dad always says what goes around comes around, and I never believed him. But this—" he yanked up both sleeves, staring at the maze of crisscrossing red lines, some still raw looking "—is all my fault? Just because you dropped him and I picked him up? I am such an idiot. What am I going to do now?"

I turned away so he wouldn't see my grin. If I let him think it was all his fault, he couldn't be mad at me for setting him up! Yes!

Kyle slumped further, head in his hands. "I deserve this! I stole it, and I deserve it—but I don't know what to do!" He looked up at me with wild eyes. "My dad can't see the beast alive—he's getting really worried that something's wrong with me. He's even thinking about taking time off work to take me to a doctor. We can't afford that!"

"Why can't your mom take you?"

"My mom? She walked out when I was three! She doesn't care what happens to us."

Guilt pressed down on me like a stegosaurus sitting on my chest. "Maybe..." I said, hesitantly.

He looked up.

"Maybe I could help," I said.

"You? Why would you help? I've only ever been awful to you, *and* I stole your dinosaur. Why would you want to help me?"

So I did what was probably the second-stupidest thing I've ever done—the first being adding the potion to my sinornithosaurus papier-mâché goop. I confessed.

"I set you up," I said, in a voice barely above a whisper. "I wanted you to steal the beast so I could get rid of him. I wanted him to hurt you."

Kyle sat very still, his mouth hanging open. Then, slowly, he closed it and said in a low tight voice, "You sicced that thing on me?" He stood and curled his hands into fists. "You made him? That monster? And then—you set me up so I would steal him, to get rid of him?"

I stood and nodded very, very slowly.

"You skunk," he shouted as he plunged his fist into my face. Pain exploded in my nose.

"You weasel," he bellowed as he drove his fist into my stomach. I doubled over, gasping.

"You miserable son-of-a-*ooomph*!"

This time, he doubled over. I stood back, my fist aching, surprised I'd been able to hit him that hard.

Suddenly he was on top of me, hammering punches down on my chest and stomach. I fought back, discovering I could throw a punch almost as well as he could, although it was easier after we rolled over and I was on top. For a little while.

We rolled and grunted and punched each other until finally we just stopped, exhausted. Kyle lay beside me, panting. My nose was bleeding and Kyle's left eye was swelling shut. He dabbed a cut on his lip with his sleeve; then he sat up, glowering at me.

I rolled over and found some tissue to sop up the blood dripping from my nose. "So, do you want to do something about that dinosaur or just keep fighting?" I asked. Of course it sounded more like "Do you vant to do sumtig about dat dinodaur?" but Kyle got the point.

He sat up, and even though he still looked really, really mad, he nodded.

"When I made him, I didn't know what he would do," I said. "I tried to get rid of him, but nothing worked. I threw him out, and I left him at the zoo. But he kept coming back."

"I know," said Kyle. "I tried to get rid of him too. But you gave him to me!"

"Ah, no, I just dropped him, and you stole him. You didn't have to take him."

"You knew I would!"

"Yeah, I did," I said.

We stared at each other, both angry. I don't know about Kyle, but I was ashamed too.

CHAPTER 10

The Monster from the Lagoon

"So what do we do?" Kyle asked.

"Huh?"

"What do we do? You said you'd help me—but what do we do?"

He didn't want to beat up on me anymore? I stood, groaning.

"Maybe we could get someone else to steal it," Kyle said.

"But who would we inflict him on?" I asked, rubbing one sore spot after another. "Who do we hate that much?"

"There are lots of people I hate," Kyle muttered.

I yanked up both his sleeves again, showing off the mazes of red lines. "Enough to do this to them?"

Kyle just shrugged, but he didn't suggest any victims.

I looked at Kyle, sitting on my bedroom floor. It was almost like having a friend over. "Maybe we could be nice to him," I said.

Kyle grunted. "How could we possibly be nice to that thing?" he asked. "Bake him a cake?"

I smiled. "Take him for a walk?"

Kyle laughed. "Bring him presents?"

We grinned and then sighed.

"We need to destroy him," Kyle said.

"But we've tried that, both of us."

"No, we've tried to get rid of him, and he always comes back. But I haven't tried to actually break him. Have you?"

I shook my head. Then I sat imagining what we might do to him. If he was just a model, we could smash him with a hammer or drop him off a building or leave him on the road to be run over. But could I do any of those things when he was alive? I shuddered. "I don't know if I could do that," I said. "It seems really gross."

Kyle frowned at me like I was chicken. Then he sighed. "Okay, what if we found a normal dinosaur way for him to die?"

"Like what?" I asked. "What dinosaur predators live around here?"

"I don't know! Maybe we could toss him into the lion cage at the zoo."

I tried to imagine that, but then I remembered what it looked like when the beast ate a chunk of meat. "No," I said, "I don't think so."

Kyle groaned. "So what if we find another way dinosaurs died?"

"Like?"

"Clarke, you have a whole room full of books about dinosaurs. One of them must talk about how dinosaurs die!"

I grinned, a little sheepish. "Yeah, that's a good idea."

Kyle grunted, and together we walked over to my bookshelf.

Kyle seemed hesitant to dive into them, so I handed him a few and grabbed a couple more for myself. We sat on the floor, surrounded by piles of books. The only listings for death were about predators and the mass extinction of dinosaurs. We had to flip right through each book to find anything about other ways dinosaurs died.

We'd read out loud a bit that might be useful, shrug if it wasn't and keep looking. On and on and on.

The piles of books got taller and taller, and we slumped lower and lower.

Then Kyle sat up straight as a book himself and said, his voice strangely intense, "Listen to this." He turned back to the book in his lap and read, struggling over the big words. "'No matter how cunning and vicious, all creatures are in constant danger from the forces of nature. The volcanoes far to the west were constantly erupting. Along with ash, they sometimes brought poisonous gas. Creatures were killed by the thousands. Many, such as the Sinornithosaurus skeleton that was recently discovered, fell or were blown into the lakes, where a blanket of fine ash covered them and preserved their remains for 120 million years."

"So?" I said, puzzled and a bit annoyed. "Where are we going to find a volcano in Calgary?"

Kyle shook his head. "We don't need a volcano. We need ash. Ash and maybe a lake."

I didn't get it. "Okay, so where do we find a lake? And ash?"

Kyle sighed. "Clarke, you're thinking dinosaur size. But we have a dinosaur model. So we only need a model-sized lake."

I shrugged.

"Like a hole in your backyard, filled with water? C'mon, use your imagination."

"A hole in the backyard? Yeah, we could dig one in the garden. Nothing's planted yet."

"And ash?" Kyle prompted.

"Uh, ash—ash. Well, we don't have a volcano," I said.

Kyle shook his head. "You idiot. You have a fireplace, don't you?"

"A fireplace?" I was feeling more and more stupid. And then, finally, I got it. "A fireplace! Of course! We'll clean out the fireplace to collect the ash, then dig a hole in the garden and fill it with water." I ran out of steam. "Then what?"

Kyle laughed. "Then we put the beast in it."

"But he'll just climb out again," I said.

"Not if your mom is watching," Kyle said, grinning. "If your mom is watching, he'll just be a model. We can put a model in a puddle, can't we?" He frowned. "Not too wussy for that, are you?"

"No," I said, feeling sheepish again. "No, this sounds fun."

We decided to do it after school the next day. Kyle hadn't the faintest idea how to catch the beast, so

I said I'd come over and help him trap it. Then we'd bring him to my house. I checked with Mom; she was thrilled. I could hear her humming as she started supper, and I knew she was thinking *Lucas has a friend, Lucas has a friend.*

Kyle lived a few blocks the other way from school, in a duplex on a busy street. A huge spruce tree filled most of the yard, shading the front window. The cement steps up to the front door were cracked and stained, and the turquoise paint on the house was peeling. Kyle pulled a key out of his backpack and unlocked the front door. I hadn't told Mom that Kyle had his own key and that his dad wouldn't be home.

The house was untidy. Not dirty, exactly, but old and worn and rumpled. A jumble of blankets had been pushed to one end of the flowered velvet sofa in their living room. On a table by the sofa was a framed photo of a smiling woman with curly red hair and blue eyes like Kyle's.

"Your mom?" I guessed.

"Yeah," Kyle said. His jaw tightened. "She lives in Vancouver."

He pushed past me into the kitchen, and I followed. The kitchen was old and dingy, with dark wooden cupboards and a fridge the color of mustard. Breakfast dishes were piled in the sink.

Kyle leaned into the fridge and emerged with a handful of raw ground beef he dropped into a bowl. "No problem getting raw burger for the beast. Dad never notices if I take some before I cook dinner."

"You cook dinner?" I asked, stunned. I didn't know anyone in grade four who could cook.

"Yeah," he said while he scrubbed his hands. "I'm the king of Hamburger Helper. Dad doesn't get home until after six, and he's dirty from work so he showers. And he's tired. If I waited for him to cook dinner, I'd starve. I'm good at Kraft dinner too, but the beast doesn't like it."

I stared at him, openmouthed.

He just shrugged and led me down the hall. He stopped in front of a closed door. "Ready?" he asked.

"Uh, is he loose in your room?" I asked, suddenly nervous.

"Of course he is," he said. "Where else would he be?"

"I kept him in my closet," I said, puzzled he hadn't figured that out.

Kyle frowned. "So that's why you aren't as scratched! My closet doors are broken. The landlord won't fix anything, and he won't pay for supplies either."

"Doesn't the beast attack you in the night? He did me, the first night."

"Oh, yeah," said Kyle, rubbing the deep scratch down the side of his face. "That's why I've been sleeping on the sofa."

I remembered the pile of blankets. "Maybe we could put the blankets over our heads," I said, "for protection. And we should wear leather gloves."

Kyle looked at me like I was nuts. "Who has leather gloves? Dad has work gloves, but he needs them. I'm not allowed to touch his tools. If he doesn't have what he needs when he needs it, he can't do his job, he doesn't get paid and we don't eat. So I don't touch his tools. But we could use the blankets."

We draped ourselves in blankets and stood at the door again, looking like Jedi knights who'd just crawled out of bed.

Kyle opened the door, and we stepped into the room.

The beast leapt at us, screeching. I jumped back, but he clawed his way up my blanket. I kicked through the blanket and he flew off, banging against the edge of Kyle's bed. While he lay on the floor, stunned, Kyle knelt beside him and waved the raw meat near his nose.

"Don't give it to him," I said. "Put it in the bag, so he'll crawl in on his own."

"Grab the bag, would you?" he asked. "I tossed it into the closet."

I rooted around in his closet, through piles of worn-out runners and old jeans. Finally I spotted the bag and grabbed it from a dark corner. It smelled even worse than when I'd had it; I gagged and hoped Mom never saw or smelled it.

The beast was growling over the bowl of meat. I snapped, "I told you not to feed him."

Kyle looked up at me with scared eyes. "If I hadn't fed him, he'd have attacked again."

I sighed and knelt beside the beast. "Help me with the bag," I said.

Kyle and I spread open the bag. Then I slid it right beside the beast. I slipped my hand under the bowl. The beast growled and shook his head at me, bits of raw meat flying from his mouth. Then he turned back to his food.

Slowly, I slid the bag under the bowl and set the bowl down inside. The beast was too focused on eating to notice; he just followed the food straight into the bag.

Carefully, Kyle and I drew up the bag around the beast. He didn't realize what was happening until we were pulling the top closed. Then, with a shriek, he struggled to get out, clawing at our hands as we tugged the bag shut. By the time we'd tied it, Kyle was bleeding and I had a new gouge across the palm of my hand.

But the beast was in the bag, and we were ready to bury it.

Kyle and I washed quickly. Then I grabbed my backpack and Kyle grabbed the beast's bag, and we walked over to my house.

We didn't talk much. We were too focused on the job to do anything but walk and think.

As soon as we got off Kyle's street, the neighborhood became nicer: not much traffic, lots of trees, well-kept houses instead of run-down duplexes. The houses were small but freshly painted, with raked and mown lawns.

My house looked really nice after Kyle's. It even smelled nicer here, fresh and green.

Mom was working in the front garden. I asked her if we could dig in the vegetable garden in the backyard.

"You want to dig the garden for me?" she said, smiling. "Oh, yeah. Any time! Well, any time before I've planted it. After that it's off-limits."

I grinned. "No problem. We just want to dig today."

I grabbed a shovel and we set to work. The soil was dug every year, so it didn't take long to start a hole. But the soil got harder the deeper we dug. Soon we were turning up chunks of pale gray clay, sticky and dense. But we kept digging, taking turns when we got tired, until we had a hole half as deep as the shovel.

Mom brought out a plate of double chocolate cookies and two glasses of milk. "You guys are working so hard, I thought you might need a snack." We ate the cookies almost as fast as the beast had eaten his meat. Then we got back to work.

I dragged over the garden hose. When the hole was filled with water, we went in search of ash.

Our fireplace has a tiny door on the outside of the chimney for cleaning out the ash. I got the little shovel from beside the fireplace and a plastic bag, and Kyle and I shoveled out a winter's worth of gray ash and black coals. Kyle held the bag while I shoveled. Each time I dropped a shovelful of ash into the bag, it rose up in a white cloud, coating Kyle's hands and leaving him choking. I finally learned to slide it off the shovel really slowly, and Kyle learned to hold the bag close to the little door and far from his face. Pretty soon we had a bag full of ash and a clean fireplace.

We carried the ash back to the vegetable patch and set it beside our lake. Except it wasn't a lake anymore; the water had drained out, leaving a muddy hole. We liked the idea of a mud pit, so while I filled the hole with water, Kyle stirred the dirt with a broken branch, making a thick, dark soup.

Mom wandered over to take a look, and I realized that was the perfect time to take out the beast. She stood near the hole, holding a bucket filled with dead leaves and gardening tools. I hid the bag behind some raspberry canes so she wouldn't see how gross it had become. The beast clawed at my hands as I untied the bag. Then he became still as I turned toward Mom. Before she could stop me, I took what she thought was my beautiful feathered dinosaur model and dropped him into the mud. Mom gasped.

Kyle grabbed the bag of ash and spoke in a low, rumbly voice. "The beast fell into a pit of mud. On a normal day he might have been able to escape—but on this day—this fateful day—the great volcano Kylealuke erupted, burying the dinosaur's world in ash."

Mom started to laugh.

Then Kyle turned the bag of ash upside down and dumped. Wind caught the ash and blew it into our faces. We choked and jumped back and watched as maybe half of it settled on the surface of the mud.

Mom jumped back too. "Oh, you guys—this is gross!" But she was so pleased I was being gross outside with a friend instead of sitting alone in my room that she smiled when she said it. And she didn't say a thing about the ash and clay in her garden.

Then Kyle added, still using his voice of doom, "Now, we wait, to see if the dinosaur can survive this terrible disaster."

Mom shrugged. "Well, it's not going to crawl out on its own, is it?"

I choked and turned away so she couldn't see my face. Kyle kicked me and turned back to the ash pit. When we just stood there, waiting, Mom got bored and went back to work.

Kyle and I stood frozen, watching, waiting for movement, for some sign of life. We knew he wouldn't be able to move until Mom was gone, so perhaps now he would crawl out. But he didn't. The ash settled in a gray layer, swirling in little whirlpools when the wind gusted, but nothing rose from below.

I smiled, just a little. "Maybe this'll really work," I muttered.

"Just wait," said Kyle, but he smiled too.

"The longer he's down there, the more likely he'll die," I said. "He can't breathe mud." I was barely breathing myself, waiting, hoping.

And still nothing moved. We smiled at each other. As the ash pit stayed quiet, we started to grin.

"We've done it," I whispered. "We've done it!"

Kyle's eyes started to shine. "You really think so?"

"Oh, yeah. He couldn't possibly live that long without air!"

And then the mud burped. Kyle and I jumped back in horror. He hadn't died—he was still alive—how could that be? He really must be some kind of monster. We stared at the pile of ash; my stomach felt like a mud pit.

As we watched, the ash shifted, the mud burbled and one foot emerged.

Just like in a horror movie, one arm reached out, coated in mud and ash, then another foot and then the head. The beast looked all around until he spotted us. He stared, his eyes filled with hate.

CHAPTER 11

howweirdcanyouget.com

Kyle and I looked at each other in horror. The beast was alive!

He crawled up the lip of the mud pit, through the ash, and hung on the side of the pool, coated in black ooze, staring at us. I stared back, unable to move, to speak, to think. Finally Kyle elbowed me.

"What should we do?" he whispered.

I hadn't a clue. I was so tired of the beast, so tired of fighting him. But when he lifted his head and started to roar, I knew I had to do something.

"Mom," I bellowed. Then I whispered to Kyle, "If Mom's here, he'll be a model, and we can put him in the bag." Then I yelled again. "Mom!"

She came running. "What is it?" she said, panting slightly. She looked all around, trying to figure out what the panic was.

"Look," I said. "He's alive!"

She took one look at the beast, frozen at the side of the pond, mud-caked arms and head emerging from the goo, and started to laugh. "You guys are so weird," she said as she turned away.

I made a face at Kyle to keep her talking. Kyle made a face back; he didn't want to do it. *C'mon*, I mimed. *You have to.* At least that's what I tried to say with waving hands and scrunched-up face.

Kyle sighed and called out, "Mrs. Clarke?"

Mom turned and took a few steps back toward us. "Yes, Kyle?"

I bent down to grab the leather bag.

"Um, could I get the recipe for your double chocolate cookies? They're really good."

"Your mom likes to bake?"

He shook his head. "I live with my dad."

Mom nodded. "Sure. I'll photocopy the recipe for you."

While they were talking, I scooped up the beast and dropped him into the leather bag, struggling to keep the beast in view of Mom, but the bag out of her sight.

Kyle and I dragged ourselves inside and scrubbed off the mud. We went back outside when Mom called us to clean the ash and clay out of her garden. Then she sent us in to scrub again and have a few more cookies. Finally we headed upstairs to figure out a new plan.

Kyle dropped the bag on the floor and shut my door, while I flipped on the radio to cover the beast's shrieks of rage. Kyle and I flopped on my bed, side by side.

"What are we going to do now?" Kyle grumbled.

I groaned. "No idea."

We both sighed.

"How did we get into this in the first place?" Kyle asked, shaking his head.

"All from some stupid website," I moaned.

Kyle sat up suddenly. "Show me."

"What?"

"Show me the website. Maybe it'll give us some ideas."

We raced downstairs into the office. Kyle stopped at the doorway to look around, but I ignored Mom's desk and filing cabinets and went straight to the computer table. I sat at the keyboard, and Kyle pulled up another chair. I logged on and got onto the Internet. In just

a few minutes the home page for howweirdcanyouget.
com was loading.

Kyle watched in silence. I glanced over as I waited.
He had a funny look on his face. "What?" I asked.

"I wish I had a computer at home," he said softly.
"You have no idea how lucky you are."

I shrugged, not wanting to make a big deal of it.

Once we were on the website, Kyle and I started to
skim through the ads.

"There's the kit I ordered," I said, pointing at the
roaring dinosaur over the text. "Make a Dinosaur
Come to Life, nineteen ninety-five."

We kept going, muttering as we read the ads.

"Turn your skateboard into a hoverboard."

"Talking masks."

"Hey, how about this one?" I said with an excited
squeak. "*Dinosaur Too Lively?*" The picture with this
ad was of a dinosaur rising up on its hind legs, claws
slashing, mouth open in what looked like a gigantic
roar.

Kyle leaned forward to read the small print. "What
is alive will be still, but only if sprayed, when alive, by
the creator or owner. Only sixty-nine ninety-five."

"What?" I said, indignant. "Twenty bucks to get into
trouble, and seventy to get out? What a rip-off!"

Kyle laughed. "Kind of clever, don't you think? It's not like we won't buy it!" Then he paused. "You can buy it, can't you?"

"I don't have seventy dollars," I said. "I have some allowance money, but I spent all my birthday money on the last kit and a book. I spend all my money on dinosaur stuff. How much do you have?"

Kyle flushed. I stared. I'd never seen him turn red before. He turned away and mumbled, "I spent all my money too. I don't have a thing."

"Nothing?" I asked, not believing him. He must have some change in a piggy bank, at least. "C'mon, Kyle, we have to do this. I can't pay for it all."

He muttered something.

"What?" I asked.

"I don't have any money," he said, his voice tight. "I don't get an allowance, and I have NO money."

I just sat there, staring. "No allowance?"

Kyle shook his head. "My dad doesn't make enough. He struggles just to pay rent and buy food. So no nice house, no computer, no allowance. Get it?" He sounded angry.

And then, finally, I got it. Now it was my turn to flush. I reached around the computer to turn on the printer so Kyle wouldn't see my face.

"Okay," I said while I printed out the ad. "Let's count up what I have and then figure out how we can earn some more. Maybe Mom will pay us to dig the rest of the garden."

Dad came home while we were logging out. He poked his head in to say hi and tried to hide his surprise that I wasn't alone. I heard him in the kitchen while we were walking up the stairs.

"Lucas has a friend over?"

"Mmm," Mom answered. "They made a huge mess in the garden, killing off his new feathered dinosaur. It's the first time he's ever damaged one of his models. But they were having so much fun I just fed them more cookies."

"See," Dad said, "I told you he'd find a friend."

I hurried Kyle up the stairs, hoping he hadn't heard any of it, but I could tell by the red on the back of his neck that he understood too much.

I emptied my piggy bank on my bed, and Kyle and I counted out my change. $17.32. I sighed and shook my head. "I guess we'll be digging," I said.

As we left my room, I saw Kyle hesitate for just a moment and then stop to pick up the beast's bag.

"You can leave him here," I said, hating every word I spoke.

Kyle shook his head. "No, I don't have any money, but I can do this."

I followed him down the stairs, blinking. "Thanks, Kyle."

We headed into the kitchen, where Mom and Dad were cooking dinner together. "Mom, Kyle and I need some money for dinosaur stuff. Would you pay us to dig the vegetable garden for you?"

I tried to sound excited about the possibility. She smiled down at me and ruffled my hair. "Sure. Just not as deep as your lake today, okay? I don't want any clay mixed in with my soil." Then she turned to Kyle. "Do you want to stay for dinner, Kyle? Chicken stir-fry!"

Kyle looked surprised and then uncomfortable. "I'd like to, but my dad will be expecting me."

"Another time, then," Mom said with a smile.

Kyle nodded and smiled back, just a little. I knew he was thinking about getting home to cook dinner for his dad.

As he left, the bag over his shoulder, I told him to wait while I dashed into the garage. When I came back, I handed him an old pair of leather gloves. "Mom buys a new pair every year. Just watch out for the holes in the fingertips."

Kyle and I worked every day after school. We dug the garden and helped Mom clean out the flower beds. When she saw how hard we were working, she let me order the kit on her credit card. "But it's coming to me, and I won't let you have it until you've paid me back, in full," she warned.

Then she sent us out to turn the compost. When it rained, we cleaned the garage. We washed the van and then vacuumed and cleaned it inside. Every day she had a new job for us, and every day she marked off $5.00 for each of us against the loan.

On Friday, when Kyle and I got home from school, dreading our next job, Mom just smiled and handed us a package. "Look what arrived today!"

"We still owe you a little," I said. My hands trembled as I held the box.

"I know. But you guys have really impressed me with how hard you've worked, so the last bit is my treat."

I grinned. "Thanks, Mom! You have no idea how great this is!" Then Kyle and I raced each other up the stairs.

CHAPTER 12

Onion Breath

We sat on my bed and unwrapped the box. It was larger than the last one, like a medium-sized shoebox. It was wrapped in brown paper and thoroughly taped. We struggled with the tape; finally I grabbed some scissors and cut it. Then we set the box between us on the bed and looked at each other. Together, we lifted off the lid.

All we saw was scrunched-up paper. But when we pulled it out, we found a plastic spray bottle filled with a milky white liquid.

"What is this?" Kyle asked, holding it up to the window. It was so dense we couldn't see light through it at all, and yet it didn't seem that thick when we just looked into the bottle. When we tipped it, it moved like water.

I rummaged around under the rest of the scrunched-up paper and found an instruction sheet. I unfolded it and started to read out loud:

Dinosaur Too Lively?
What is alive will be still,
but only if sprayed, when alive,
by the creator/owner.

We glanced at each other. "I'm the creator, and you're the owner, so I guess we both have to do it," I said.

Kyle nodded. He took the sheet from me and continued reading:

Spray all parts.
Warning: It is essential not to spray
anything you want to be able to move.
Cover your skin.

I could feel my eyes bugging out as I listened. Kyle suddenly looked pale.

"Are you sure we should do this?" I asked.

"Clarke, nothing else has worked," he said. "I think we both have to do it, and no one else can help us or he won't be alive when we spray him." He gulped. "But I think we'd better do it very carefully!"

So Kyle and I collected gear. Long-sleeved shirts, pants, runners, bike helmets, gardening gloves, bandanas for our faces, ski goggles and a second spray bottle. We stuffed everything into a gym bag, told Mom we were going to Kyle's for a bit before dinner and headed to his house.

We put on our gear in Kyle's dingy kitchen. We helped each other tie on the bandanas, anchored them with the ski goggles and pulled up our collars to protect our necks. We looked silly, like four year olds pretending to be knights. We laughed at each other, but not very hard.

The trickiest bit was pouring half the solution into the second spray bottle. Kyle didn't have a funnel, so he just poured very, very carefully. He worked at the sink, with gloves on and Baggies over the gloves, but we still held our breath while he poured. Three drops crawled down the outside of the bottle. I carefully wiped them off with a paper towel and stuffed the paper towel into a garbage bag. Then we stood, looking at each other, neither of us wanting to start.

"We can do this," I said, trying to sound brave.

"Sure we can," said Kyle. "We can beat one weeny little dinosaur."

I could tell from the look in his eyes that he didn't really think the beast was weeny, and neither did I, but we were both ready to pretend.

"Yeah," I said. "We're much tougher than he is." I took a deep breath and let out my best dinosaur roar.

Kyle looked shocked; then he grinned. "I can roar louder than that!" He threw back his head and let loose a thundering roar that echoed around the room. I joined in, the two of us sounding like rampaging dinosaurs. Then we heard an echoing cry from down the hall. We looked at each other, suddenly silent and weak-kneed.

We gave each other a final check, tucking sleeves into gloves and adjusting our bandanas; then we picked up our spray bottles and walked down the hall to Kyle's bedroom.

Kyle's room was disgusting. It smelled like rotting meat, and the floor was covered in dirty clothes and torn papers. I couldn't tell how much mess was normal and how much was from the beast. I could hear him banging in a bottom drawer.

"I figured a drawer would work almost as well as a closet," Kyle whispered, "so I put food and water inside it. The beast leaps around the room in a rage, and when he gets hungry he goes into the drawer. Then I slam it shut."

I knelt by the drawer and held out my spray bottle. Kyle stood directly in front of the drawer, legs wide, mouth firm, spray bottle pointed at the drawer. Then he nodded.

Slowly, I opened the drawer, just a little. The beast screeched and clawed at the open edge. We both started squirting. It took a few pumps for my bottle to start to work. Then white spray flew from it. It hit the beast's claw as he groped for a way out of the drawer. We heard a slight hissing when the spray hit his foot; suddenly, the foot stopped. It just totally stopped, like it was frozen or something. The beast screamed and pulled his frozen foot back into the drawer.

Kyle and I glanced at each other, wondering what to do next. The beast screamed again and threw his body against the drawer. The drawer tipped open just enough for the beast to climb out, screeching and leaping on three legs.

We jumped back and took aim again. We started squeezing frantically, but he moved so fast he was hard to hit. Kyle and I danced around the room, trying to keep out of his reach and spray the beast but not each other.

It was a good thing there were no plants in the room. Spray went everywhere. Whenever it hit something not alive, it was like spraying milk. But when the spray touched the beast, we could hear hissing.

I felt the spray hit my helmet, and I got Kyle in the back. But we were covered and the beast wasn't.

The beast leapt at my legs, and in his fury he climbed right up my pants. I jumped back in a panic and hit at him with the base of my spray bottle, trying to make him let go. Finally he dropped to the floor, shrieking, and gathered himself up for another leap. Kyle and I sprayed and sprayed and sprayed until we had no spray left and were pumping air.

It took us a few moments to realize we were both pumping uselessly. Gradually our hands slowed and stopped. We stared down at the beast. He looked like he was about to leap at us in fury, but he didn't move. We glanced at each other and leaned down for a better look. He still didn't move. Kyle touched the beast with his runner, the beast tipped over, like he was just a model again.

But he was a much better model than I had made. Much more lifelike. Much more ferocious-looking. And he still had a nasty gleam in his eye.

We kept glancing at him while we cleaned up. Kyle worried about all the spray in his room, but once it was dry, it didn't seem to do anything. We tested it—Kyle touched the very tip of one finger to a dry spot and then rubbed his finger. It was fine, but we both found spots that weren't. Kyle's right sleeve had slipped up his arm, and he had a numb patch just above his glove. And when Kyle had sprayed my helmet, some dripped onto the edge of my left ear. It left a little numb patch. I ran my finger up and down the edge of my ear, from feeling to numbness to feeling again.

Once we'd cleaned up everything, Kyle and I stood staring down at the beast. It felt like he was looking at us, even though we knew he wasn't. We could still feel his malevolence.

"What do we do with him?" I asked. "I don't want him!"

"Me neither! I could send him to my mom," Kyle said with a nasty grin. "Let her live with him!"

I shuddered. "No, that's too mean," I said. "Even when he is just a model."

"So what do we do?"

"He's so nasty-looking, no one would want him," I said, looking down at him. "Unless they really, really loved ferocious dinosaurs."

"So who loves dinosaurs even more than you do?" Kyle asked.

"Well, no one," I said. "No one I know of. Except—" I stood there, thinking.

"What?"

"Well, the Tyrrell Museum collects dinosaurs. And they must really, really love them. Maybe we could send him there."

Kyle started to laugh. "And if he came back to life, they'd know just what to do!"

So we found a box, packed up the beast and mailed him to the Royal Tyrrell Museum of Paleontology, Drumheller, Alberta. No return address.

Monday morning at school, Kyle and I met up first thing.

"I brought a book for you to look at," I said. I groped around in my backpack and pulled out a book on feathered dinosaurs. He laughed when I showed it to him.

Soon a couple of other kids were edging closer to take a look. They gathered around to see the pictures. Then they started peppering us with questions.

"It's Luke's book. Ask him," Kyle said.

And they did. And they called me Luke. Not Clarke or Lark or even Lucas like my mom and dad. Just Luke. I liked it.

Then I saw Kyle getting pushed back from the book. I said something about the sounds dinosaurs might have made, and then I nodded at Kyle. "You should hear Kyle's dinosaur roar," I said.

They turned to him, their faces a weird mix of curiosity and fear. When he roared, their nervousness changed to shaky laughter, replaced by real laughter as we all roared.

After school, Kyle came over to my house. Mom had cookies waiting.

"Hi, Kyle," she said, smiling. "It's good to see you."

He smiled back.

We ate as many cookies as we could before Mom stopped us; then we took Stegy outside.

Kyle wandered around the front yard for a few minutes to let Stegy graze in the back garden; then he joined me. As soon as he came around the corner, Stegy quit moving.

"It's hard to believe he's real," Kyle said, watching Stegy sitting in the garden.

"Smell his breath," I said.

"Huh?"

"Smell his breath. He's been grazing on chives. See where they're all chewed down? Chives smell like onions, so smell his breath."

Kyle picked him up and took a deep breath. "Eew! You're right! This is so cool!"

"I could make you one," I said.

"You could?"

"I have enough potion left for one more. But it would have to be a nice one, like Stegy."

"But how would it be real for me?"

"You'd have to steal it, I guess."

Kyle looked uncomfortable. "I—uh—I don't want to steal from you."

"Well it won't work if I say you can take it, will it?"

Kyle grinned. "Right. So go make yourself another dinosaur!"

"Or maybe," I said, "we could make it together. Then it would be alive for both of us from the beginning."

Kyle grabbed Stegy and we raced upstairs to look through my books to choose a dinosaur.

"We could make another stegosaurus," I said. "Then they could play together."

"Who could?" asked Kyle.

"Your dinosaur and Stegy. Oh, except Stegy could never be real for you." I sighed. "It would be so much more fun if they could both be real for both of us." I looked around. "Where is Stegy?"

Kyle turned a page of his book. "Oh, I put him down somewhere," he said, shrugging.

I couldn't see him, but as I was looking around, I noticed Kyle's backpack moving. "Kyle, what's in your backpack?" I asked.

Kyle flushed. He leaned down to open it and lifted out Stegy. "I thought if I stole him, we could both play with him."

I grinned as I watched Stegy sniffing Kyle's hand. "Great idea," I said.

While we were looking through books for photos of stegosauruses, the printout from howweirdcanyouget. com fell out of a book. We'd printed the page with the ad we wanted; other ads filled the page. I glanced at them and started to laugh. "Hey, listen to this. 'Make your bicycle fly.'"

"Oh, yeah," said Kyle. He slid over to read over my shoulder. "'Talk to your fish.' Ever wanted to own fish?" he asked.

"'Live Specimens of Mythical Creatures'—ooh, that would be cool!" Kyle and I looked at each other and grinned. "But let's start with a dinosaur," I said.

Born in Edmonton, Maureen Bush was raised in Edmonton and Calgary. She has worked as a public involvement consultant and trained as a mediator. Her first book was *The Nexus Ring* (Coteau Books, 2007). Maureen lives in Calgary with her husband and two daughters.

Addison Addley and the Things that Aren't There

Melody DeFields McMillan

978-1-55143-949-5
$7.95 • 96 pp

Ten Thumb Sam

Rachel Dunstan Muller

978-1-55143-699-9
$7.95 • 128 pp

Racing for Diamonds

Anita Daher

978-1-55143-675-3
$7.95 • 128 pp

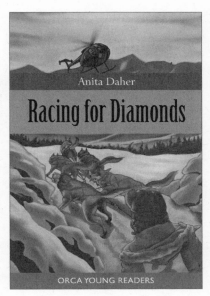

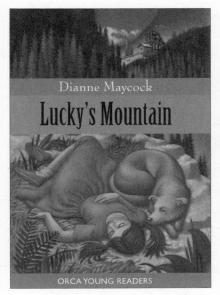

Lucky's Mountain

Diane Maycock

978-1-55143-682-1
$7.95 • 112 pp